A DEATH DEMANDED

A FERNANDO LOPEZ SANTA FE MYSTERY

A DEATH DEMANDED

A FERNANDO LOPEZ SANTA FE MYSTERY

JAMES C. WILSON

SUNSTONE
PRESS
SANTA FE

Sunstone books may be purchased for educational, business, or sales promotional use.
For information please write: Special Markets Department, Sunstone Press,
P.O. Box 2321, Santa Fe, New Mexico 87504-2321.
Printed on acid-free paper
∞
eBook: 978-1-61139-761-1

Library of Congress Cataloging-in-Publication Data

Names: Wilson, James C., 1948- author.
Title: A death demanded / James C. Wilson.
Description: Santa Fe : Sunstone Press, 2025. | Series: Fernando Lopez
    Santa Fe mystery | Summary: "An investigation of the murder of a Santa
    Fe gallery owner becomes more complicated when former private
    investigator Fernando Lopez discovers the victim was a notorious sexual
    predator who everyone despised and wanted dead"-- Provided by publisher.

Identifiers: LCCN 2024059045 | ISBN 9781632937407 (paperback ; acid-free
    paper) | ISBN 9781611397611 (epub)
Subjects: LCGFT: Detective and mystery fiction. | Novels.
Classification: LCC PS3623.I58485 D44 2025 | DDC 813/.6--dc23/eng/20241216
LC record available at https://lccn.loc.gov/2024059045

WWW.SUNSTONEPRESS.COM
SUNSTONE PRESS / POST OFFICE BOX 2321 / SANTA FE, NM 87504-2321 /USA
(505) 988-4418

"There had never been a death more foretold."
—Gabriel Garcia Marquez, *Chronicle of a Death Foretold*

THE KILLING

The sound of a key fumbling in the lock of the front door woke Sonny Davis from a fitful sleep. He groaned when he opened his eyes to a pounding headache. He was sprawled over the Taos sofa at his Athena Gallery on Canyon Road. Not again. Lately he'd been falling asleep after sex with his chippies. Getting too old for these after work trysts with the young women he hired on staff. Which one was it tonight? Becca or Angelica or maybe Mary Margaret? No, he remembered now that it wasn't one of his regulars. He'd hooked up with a woman named Jessica, or maybe Jessamyn, one of the day waitresses at the La Fonda bar, a nice piece but a little long in the tooth for his taste, which ran young.

Sonny groaned again, thinking about Jessica or Jessamyn. Hard to tell the bimbos apart, really. One as good as another. This feckin' country. Lousy football and cold women, no passion in any of them. Like rag dolls. Aye, he should have stayed in England. He would have if he hadn't busted up his knee playing for Portsmouth and been forced to migrate to the States to extend his career playing for piss-poor American teams like FC Cincinnati. That ended his playing career once and for all. Welcome to life without soccer.

Sonny noticed the dark windows. What time was it anyway? He saw his watch on the floor with his clothes. He reached over and grabbed his trousers when he heard the key enter the lock with a loud click. Shite! Who could be coming here at this late hour? His ex-wife Athena Loering no longer had a key after he had the lock changed. Sole possession of the gallery was the one thing his worthless lawyer had managed to get from the bitch. Must be one of his three chippies. Come for a wee bit of a nightcap? That made Sonny smile with confidence.

They can't stay away from me cock, none of them. He might be a washed up professional soccer player with a pot-belly and a taste for the drink, but he hadn't lost his ability to satisfy the women. No, he hadn't lost that. And he didn't need any damned Viagra!

Sonny pulled on his trousers and shuffled barefoot and bare-chested across the room to his desk, where an empty bottle of cheap champagne remained from his frolic with Jessica or Jessamyn. He gulped down half a glass that one of them had left on the desk. By that time the intruder was opening the door. He heard the heavy wooden door creak on its hinges, moaning like a ghost. Almost sounded like the door was in pain. He made a mental note to oil the feckin' door tomorrow.

Entering the front room, Sonny bumped into one of the counters in the gallery. He couldn't see a damned thing in the darkness. Then he saw something that made him jump. A dark shadow framed by a slice of light coming through a side window. A masked figure wearing a hoodie. Man or woman, he couldn't tell. The hooded face was lost in the darkness.

"Hello, darlin'... come on back," Sonny intoned, figuring it must be one of his chippies, in spite of the hoodie. Maybe she felt like a little role-playing tonight: abduction and bondage?

Then the figure raised its right arm slowly. A metal object in its right hand glinted in the half-light. "You pig!"

Sonny spotted the pistol just as it exploded: Pop!

He felt a burst of fire in his belly. Glancing down, he saw a dark liquid oozing out of an open wound.

Sonny staggered to his side, trying to spin around and run. Instead he fell to the floor and began crawling away on his hands and knees.

The shrouded figure laughed at his efforts to escape. It followed him into his office. Aiming the pistol, the figure fired twice, the bullets striking him in the back: Pop! Pop!

Suddenly Sonny lost all feeling in his arms and legs, falling flat on his face. He tasted blood in his mouth and then nothing.

Private Investigator Fernando Lopez had been retired for only a month and was already bored out of his mind. He'd closed his office on Canyon Road and returned the key to his friend and landlord Ruby Montez, who owned the gallery next door and had never charged him rent. Now he worked from home, having decided to take an occasional case as a 'fixer.' He'd moved his work files to his private study in their home on Acequia Madre Street. He figured a home office would work just fine, except he missed all his artist friends on Canyon Road, as crazy as they were. This morning Estelle, his wife, had already gone to work, so he was sitting outside on his patio by himself enjoying the fresh Spring air while reading the *Santa Fe Independent* and drinking his third or fourth cup of coffee, he'd lost track. The older he got, the more coffee he drank.

The *Independent's* lead story concerned yesterday's murder of the current owner of Athena Gallery, Sonny Davis. Fernando was all too familiar with Sonny's history. A former soccer player from Ireland, Sonny had played professional soccer in England before breaking a knee and emigrating to Cincinnati, Ohio, to coach FC Cincinnati, the city's Major League Soccer team. In Cincinnati Sonny married an older and very wealthy dowager, Athena Doering. The two of them moved to Santa Fe and opened Athena Gallery on Canyon Road, where Sonny turned out to be a notorious drunk and sexual predator, as well as a wife-beater. A real piece of shit that pretty much everyone in Santa Fe despised.

Now, according to the *Independent*, Sonny had been found shot to death on the floor of his Athena Gallery. Fernando doubted there would be many tears shed for old Sonny, given his reputation. Sonny's wife Athena had given him Athena Gallery in a nasty divorce settlement last year. Sonny wanted more, but Athena had employed Fernando to talk some sense into Sonny and get him to sign the divorce papers. Which Fernando did, making Sonny an offer he couldn't refuse—with a little help from his handy Smith & Wesson.

Since then Fernando had begun to enjoy his work as a fixer. After thirty years on the Santa Fe Police Department and another eight as a private investigator, he found that as a fixer he had more freedom and more wriggle-room, so to speak. He could take care of business unfettered and unconstrained by the legality of his work. He liked that word, unconstrained. And he didn't even need an office. Better to keep the business on the down-low, out of public sight.

When his cell phone buzzed on the bench next to him, he saw his friend Ruby's name on the screen. He hadn't spoken to Ruby since he removed the last few items from his former office a couple of weeks ago. "Ruby—what's up?" he answered.

"Hey, Fernando," Ruby said. "I need your help. Did you see the *Independent*'s article about the Sonny Davis shooting this morning?"

"Yeah, just finished it," Fernando said.

"Well, the person of interest they mentioned is me," Ruby said. "I'm calling from the Washington Avenue Police Station."

Fernando could hardly believe what he'd heard. "What? Did you shoot Sonny Davis?"

"No, I didn't have that honor, but there's probably a hundred women around Santa Fe who would have loved to shoot the bastard," Ruby responded. "As you well know, my friend."

"So how did you get involved?" Fernando asked, not understanding.

Ruby sighed at the other end. "It's a long story. I'm coming over to tell you all about it as soon as one of these goons gives me a ride back to my house. They pulled me out of bed, wouldn't even let me drive myself down to the station."

"Well, you better get a lawyer right away," Fernando said.

"I did, I called Raoul Garcia," Ruby said. "I have an appointment with him this afternoon. Wait...here comes Manny to take me home. I'll be at your house shortly."

Fernando clicked off, glad that his wife Estelle had already left for work at the Saint Francis Immigrant Outreach Program, a church nonprofit that delivered food and clothing to the growing immigrant community in Santa Fe, a Sanctuary City. Estelle and Ruby did not like each other. Not one bit. Estelle referred to Ruby as Fernando's girlfriend. Ruby ignored Estelle.

He took his cell phone and coffee cup into the house. He and Estelle had purchased their 1920s adobe on Acequia Madre Street early in their marriage. They'd preserved the small adobe pretty much as it was when they bought it, except for minor modernizations. He took great pride in preserving this small piece of history on a street blighted by gentrification. Up and down Acequia Madre wealthy newcomers had bought and remodeled the houses into million-dollar mansions. The over-class, he called them, rich people who had turned Santa Fe into Disneyland Southwest. As a result long-time Santa Feans could no longer afford to live in Santa Fe. The median price of a house in Santa Fe County was approaching one million dollars. He didn't consider himself a class warrior, but clearly something had to be done. The economic disparities had become obscene.

Though he worried about Ruby's notoriously hot temper and wicked tongue, Fernando was relieved to hear that she'd called Raoul Garcia, the best criminal lawyer in the state of New Mexico. Ruby was no stranger to Legal troubles—or any other brand of trouble, for that matter. Most recently she and her sister Tessa had run afoul of the law when the two of them, armed, had terrorized the Abiquiu area looking for the man who shot and killed Tessa's late husband, Andy Dejon. Fortunately the two of them had never found the murderer or harmed anyone in their search.

Sometimes Fernando wondered if it was more than a coincidence that both Ruby and Tessa's husbands were murdered. Both women seemed to attract bad luck and bad husbands, although Tessa, the younger sister, wasn't quite as wild or as ferocious as Ruby. Or so he thought.

He and Ruby went back a long way, even before he met and married Estelle. Always prickly, Ruby wore her bad attitude with pride. To her, it was a badge of honor. Her in-your-face personality put off many people but had made her a force in Santa Fe politics for over two decades. A potter by trade, Ruby had risen through the ranks of *La Raza* to become the most progressive member of City Council ever. Back in the 1990s she fought tooth and nail against all the greedy developers who wanted to turn downtown Santa Fe into one big shopping mall. She led rallies, marches, protests, sit-ins, and if you believed the rumors, a fire-bombing or two.

She lost, of course. The tide of gentrification sweeping over Santa Fe during those years hollowed out the city. Gone were most of the people whose families had lived in Santa Fe for generations. Increasingly higher home values and property taxes priced out all who couldn't afford the million-dollar homes. After two tumultuous terms on City Council lecturing, berating, cajoling, and threatening the other members, she said 'fuck it' and retired to the pottery co-op she owned and ran with a number of other potters, most of them women.

Still she refused to be silenced. She made it a point to attend most Council meetings and give the members a piece of her mind. Every one of them feared Ruby's tirades. Occasionally her anger would get the better of her language and she would be asked to leave. Once a few years back City Council banned her for a year, but her lawyer, Raoul Garcia, sued their asses and got her reinstated in her front row seat staring down the Council.

Over the years he and Ruby had always been friendly, probably because they felt the same way about gentrification and Santa Fe politics in general. That is, they usually ended up on the losing side. So it goes.

Fernando looked around the kitchen, deciding to make another pot of coffee for Ruby's visit. He rinsed out his coffee pot and then added coffee and water. He waited until he heard a car come down Acequia Madre and turn into his driveway. He checked to make sure it was Ruby's Honda Accord and then hit the brew button on the automatic coffee maker. By the time Ruby knocked on his kitchen door, Fernando had a cup of coffee waiting for her on the kitchen table.

Seeing Ruby always cheered Fernando. With her long black hair now streaked with gray, her black bedroom eyes, and her ironic smile, Ruby was a knock-out. She wore black tights and a maroon sweater that accented every curve.

"Oh...thanks," Ruby said, stepping inside and seeing the cup of coffee waiting for her at the kitchen table.

Fernando took a seat across the table from Ruby.

"So what's the story? Why are you a person of interest in the Sonny Davis murder?" Fernando asked, sipping his coffee.

Ruby shook her head and ignored the coffee. "Because the gun that killed Sonny happens to be registered to my ex-husband Jimmy Mackey, which I inherited. They found the gun next to Sonny's body. I'm sure my fingerprints are all over it. Tessa's too probably."

"You mean that old Glock pistol you two were waving around up in Abiquiu, threatening people you thought might have killed Tessa's husband?"

Ruby gave him a dirty look, as if telling him not to bring up that debacle.

"I told you to put that thing away...that it was just going to get you in trouble," Fernando said.

"Yeah, but I don't want to hear a lecture from you now, okay?" Ruby responded. "I haven't even seen that gun since Abiquiu. I don't know what the hell happened to it. Maybe Tessa moved it, I haven't had a chance to ask her because Manny and those other bastards dragged me out of bed this morning and hauled me off to the police station like a common criminal."

"Is that what you told the police?" Fernando asked. "That you hadn't seen the gun recently?"

"Yeah, because it's the truth!" Ruby shot back, her face reddening.

"I'm just trying to help," Fernando replied. "Have you had any break-ins at the gallery? Could someone have stolen it?"

"No, not recently," Ruby said.

Fernando paused, taking another sip of coffee. He tried to figure out a way to ask his next question without infuriating Ruby. "What about Tessa? She moved in with you, yes?"

Ruby shook her head. "Only for a few days. Now she's thinking of moving in with Blaine."

"Blaine?" Fernando asked, surprised. This was news to him. Blaine Rogers owned Picasso and Company gallery on Canyon Road. A wild, eccentric artist himself, Blaine was known for his odd behavior and crazy escapades, as well as his drinking. He and Ruby were legends at El Farol because of their drinking capacity and their knack for starting shouting matches and occasional brawls.

"Yeah, I know," Ruby said. "I told her to stay away from that asshole, but you know Tessa, she has a mind of her own. She says she might be in love with him, if you can believe that. Hah! Blaine's about as monogamous as I am!"

"Okay, but even if she doesn't live with you, she had access to the Glock, right?" Fernando asked.

"What are you suggesting—that Tessa killed Sonny?" Ruby responded, her face bright red now. "Why would Tessa shoot Sonny? She wouldn't get near that wife-beating bastard. She knew how he treated his wife."

Fernando nodded, hoping to ease Ruby's anger. "So then, what do you want me to do? I'm not sure I understand how I can help."

"I want you to find out who killed Sonny, what do you think," Ruby said. "And fast, before they actually arrest me."

"Why, what did they tell you down at the station?" Fernando asked. "Did they take your fingerprints?"

"Yeah, they took my fingerprints," Ruby said. "Then Manny said they would be in touch. Fucking Manny! He's supposed to be a friend."

Not liking what he was hearing, Fernando asked, "Where were you the night Sonny was murdered? Do you have someone who can vouch for you?"

Ruby looked offended. "No, I don't need someone who can vouch for me because I didn't shoot Sonny. I was home alone that night."

Fernando did not respond.

"Can't you talk to Manny or something?" Ruby asked. "You know, get him off my back? You guys are best friends, right?"

Fernando laughed. Sort of. "I'll do my best, but I can't promise anything. Manny's a good cop. I'm sure he's just trying to do his job."

"Good. Then find out who killed Sonny," Ruby ordered. With that, she stood up from the table and walked out of the kitchen without looking back. She hadn't touched her coffee.

Fernando watched Ruby walk out to her car and take off fast, kicking up a small dust tornado in the gravel driveway. The woman was a force of nature.

2

Fernando watched Ruby's Honda disappear down Acequia Madre Street. As soon as the car was out of sight he sat back down at the kitchen table with his cell phone and called Manny Alvarez, who'd replaced Fernando as lead detective in the Santa Fe Police Department a few years back. Manny answered immediately and sounded agitated: "Alvarez here, what is it?"

"Manny—what's wrong?" Fernando asked.

"Oh, Fernando...it's you," Manny said, his voice relaxing a bit. "Your friend Ruby, that's what's wrong. She's driving me crazy. Again!"

Fernando laughed. "Yeah, I heard, she just left my house."

"Then you know the whole story," Manny said, sighing. "She has no explanation for why her pistol, a Glock registered to her dead ex-husband Jimmy Mackey, was found next to the body of Sonny Davis. No explanation! Even worse, her fingerprints are all over the pistol."

Fernando interrupted Manny. "But did you find other fingerprints besides Ruby's?"

"Yes, prints everywhere," Manny said. "Forensics found at least six or seven other sets of prints. But even if Ruby didn't pull the trigger, the question is did she encourage or even enlist someone else to shoot Sonny? It's her gun, right?"

"Okay, but you have a number of other potential suspects, not just Ruby," Fernando said. "Keep in mind that Sonny was not a popular figure on Canyon Road. In fact, most people hated the bastard."

"Right, I know," Manny admitted. "We're starting with whoever was with Sonny the night he was murdered. He apparently had sex with someone on the Taos sofa in his office. Forensics found a used condom and a bottle of lube on the floor, along with some of his clothes. They also found a half bottle of champagne and glasses. Looked like Sonny was having a grand old time until someone came in and shot him. We don't know the identity of Sonny's fuck buddy or if the fuck buddy was the person who shot him. In other words, we don't know much of anything at this point."

"Too many possibilities," Fernando said, mostly to himself.

"Exactly, which is why we have to round up the other people who knew and worked at the gallery for fingerprinting, starting with Tessa. We haven't been able to find her."

"Ruby said Tessa moved in with Blaine," Fernando said. "Have you tried Blaine's house, or his Picasso and Company gallery?"

"Blaine Rogers? No, that's news to me."

"Me too," Fernando said. "I don't know why any woman in their right mind would want to move in with Blaine."

"Yeah, well, there you have it," Manny said. "She's probably not in her right mind, although as I remember, she's a little more cooperative than her crazy older sister Ruby."

Fernando laughed. "Who isn't?"

"Good point," Manny said. "Believe me, the last thing I want to do is arrest Ruby on suspicion of murder. I have a meeting with the Chief this afternoon. He'll make the decision then. Gotta go."

Manny clicked off before Fernando could ask more questions.

Fernando carefully placed his cell phone on the kitchen table and sat down. Maybe he shouldn't have told Manny about Tessa living with Blaine. He would like to at least find Tessa and talk with her before the police grabbed her. To give her fair warning about what she could expect. Ruby was an old hand at dealing with the police, but Tessa not so much.

So why wait?

He quickly locked up the house and walked to his Cherokee. He drove down Acequia Madre to the Paseo and over to Canyon Road. Then he drove up Canyon Road and parked in front of Blaine's Picasso and Company gallery, just down the street from his old office. Blaine lived in a small adobe house behind the gallery, but Fernando chose the cobblestone walkway to the gallery, a large territorial style building with banks of windows in front. The walkway took him through an untended cactus garden that cried out for a little tender loving care. The cacti looked half dead, as did the stand of hollyhocks near the front porch, everything crying out for water, a precious commodity in the Southwest.

Fernando climbed up on the porch and stepped inside, hearing a bell ring when he opened the door. He didn't see Blaine or anyone else as he walked into the main gallery, where the last of Jimmy Mackey's paintings still hung on one wall, years after Ruby's ex-husband Jimmy had been murdered. Fernando stopped to admire what Jimmy referred to as his "Chopped Nudes:" outrageous paintings of female body parts protruding out of various limbs. Fernando never understood why anyone would want one of those monstrosities hanging on their living room walls, but what did he know about art? The other side wall displayed several Southwestern landscapes and a mixture of Indian themed paintings, everything from Zuñi dancers to paintings of world famous Taos Pueblo. In other words, all the tourist crap.

Fernando stopped to look at the price tags, which shocked him. They ranged in price from $2,000 for a relatively small canvas to $25,000 for the larger ones. Back in his day you could buy a house in Santa Fe for $25,000. Times had changed and not for the better.

"Blaine?" he called out, hearing his voice echo off the walls of the gallery.

"Yeah, what?" came the gruff reply from a room behind the front counter. The office, if Fernando remembered correctly.

Fernando waited but Blaine did not appear, so he walked behind the counter and into the office. Blaine sat at his desk with a bottle of tequila and a pint beer glass in front of him. The pint glass was half full of tequila.

"Jesus, Blaine, it's a little early for tequila, isn't it?" Fernando asked, noticing that Blaine wore his usual clothes, red Bermuda shorts and a white T-shirt with a fishing vest over it. Eccentric didn't even begin to describe Blaine and his choice of wardrobe, if you could call red Bermuda shorts and a white T-shirt a wardrobe, because that's all Blaine wore. Only cold weather and snow could force him to wear red sweats and a gray sweatshirt.

Blaine frowned and gave Fernando a dirty look. The big man appeared positively forlorn, morose. Unusual for Blaine, who was normally lively and energetic, if not in a full-blown manic state.

"What do you want?" Blaine asked.

"I'm looking for Tessa," Fernando said. "I need to talk to her before Manny finds her."

"Manny? Why would Manny be looking for Tessa?" Blaine shot back, getting to his feet, all six feet, five inches and two hundred fifty pounds of him. He gave Fernando the Evil Eye. The big man was intimidating enough without being upset or angry or whatever his problem happened to be at the moment.

Fernando held up his hands. "You know about the Sonny Davis murder?"

Blaine nodded.

"Well, the gun that killed Sonny was Jimmy Mackey's old Glock, the one Ruby and Tessa had been carrying around in Abiquiu," Fernando explained. "Ruby's fingerprints are all over the gun. Tessa's too, probably."

Blaine sat back down heavily, shaking his head.

"Ruby wants me to find Sonny's killer before they arrest her...or Tessa," Fernando added. "Which is why I want to talk to Tessa before Manny gets to her. Not only to warn her, but to prepare her for what Manny might ask. "

"Fuck!" Blaine shouted and smacked the desk with his huge fist. "Tessa didn't have anything to do with Sonny's murder. She was with me at El Farol that night. I can vouch for her."

"She was with you the entire evening?" Fernando asked.

"Yeah, except for a few minutes when she went up the street to get some more of her clothes at Ruby's gallery," Blaine replied.

Fernando bit his tongue. The gap would be a problem. He tried to change the subject. "So where is Tessa now, can I talk to her?"

Blaine lowered his head. "Tessa left me. She went home this morning. Took all her shit and walked out the door, just like that. I thought we had something going, but I guess not. I really fell hard for the bitch."

Fernando had to stifle a laugh. Blaine was famous for his amorous exploits, all of them fleeting. Blaine was the last person in the world who would ever be monogamous. Just as Ruby said.

"Well, that's a change," Fernando quipped "You're the one who usually hits the pavement."

Blaine gave Fernando another dirty look.

"So Tessa went back to her gallery in Abiquiu?" Fernando asked. "Is that what you mean by home?"

"Where else would it be? That's where she lives," Blaine snapped, getting a bit hot under the collar. Or more likely, half-crocked and belligerent from drinking too much tequila.

Fernando saw that it was time to get out before Blaine completely lost it. He'd seen Blaine angry and it wasn't a pretty sight. Nor was it safe to be around him. "Okay, I'll pay her a visit in Abiquiu. You want me to give her a message?"

"Yeah, tell the bitch to go fuck herself!" Blaine said angrily, but when Fernando turned to leave, Blaine took a deep breath and corrected himself. "Wait...tell her I miss her and think about her every hour of my miserable fucking existence. Ask her to please come back."

Fernando kept walking. He waved as he opened the door. "I'll do my best."

Blaine slumped over his desk, cradling his bottle of tequila as Fernando stepped outside and closed the door behind him.

3

Abiquiu used to be one of his favorite places. That was before the Jimmy Mackey manhunt and the Cowboy Jack shootout, both at Abiquiu's haunted Ghost Ranch. Rumors of the haunting began in the 1880s when the owners, the Archuleta Brothers, named the property *Rancho de los Brujos*. The brothers, notorious cattle rustlers, stole cattle and horses and hid them in the box canyon behind the ranch. They chose the name Ranch of the Witches to scare away farmers and ranchers who came looking for their stolen livestock. Rumor had it the brothers murdered those who continued to search for their animals and buried the bodies in the canyon or tossed them into wells. Ghost stories soon followed. Locals claimed to hear the voices of murdered victims in the howling winds blowing through the canyon. Some saw strange lights moving through the buildings, especially around "Ghost House," where the brothers had lived before they too met a grisly fate. One brother killed the other during an argument over booty. The surviving brother died soon after, hung by an angry posse for a life of cattle rustling and murder. Their voices joined the multitude of other ghosts howling in the wind, according to local legend.

So after sitting on his patio sipping coffee and brooding all morning, Fernando decided to go after Tessa. He would eat an early lunch and make a quick trip up to Tessa's gallery in Abiquiu, like it or not. He owed Ruby big time for all the free rent she'd given him over the years. This was the least he could do. So he gobbled down a plate of leftover enchiladas he found in the refrigerator, grabbed a bottle of water, and locked the house. One thing he didn't bring was his Smith & Wesson, figuring he wouldn't need it. He just wanted to find and talk with Tessa. Warn her and get her side of the story before Manny could get to her.

He climbed into the Cherokee and drove down to the Paseo and around to the entrance to Highway 84/285. Once out of the city limits, he began to relax. Why not enjoy the scenery, consider the road trip a mini vacation? Past the Tesuque cut-off and the Santa Fe Opera the view opened up on the Sangre de Cristo Mountains. He ignored the commercial claptrap on the Pojoaque strip and headed north to Española, where he turned left on Highway 84 to Abiquiu.

Fernando loved the scenic drive along the Chama River, where he'd hiked and fished as a young man, before family responsibilities limited his free time. He drove past the ruins of Santa Rosa de Lima and the sprawling Abiquiu Inn. Then he passed by the road leading to the village of Abiquiu on top of its mesa, where the famous Georgia O'Keeffe House looked over the highway below and the distant mesas receding to the horizon in shades of pink, gray, and white. Just beyond the turn-off to the village he came to Bode's General Store, where several cars were parked out front of the popular store and meeting place. Finally he slowed down approaching a collection of storefront shops along the highway. The last of the shops was Tessa's Abiquiu Fine Art, an old adobe structure with a flat tin roof reflecting the sunlight. The gallery's cracked stucco and peeling blue windowsills made the building look ancient.

Fernando saw the vandalism as soon as he pulled up in front of the gallery. Someone had spray-painted in huge red letters across the front of the gallery a few choice words that were hardly flattering: 'Bitch,' 'Bruja,' and 'Puta." In addition, several windows had been broken out, leaving gaping black holes in the front and side of the building. Fernando knew Tessa had more than her share of enemies in Abiquiu. That started when she and Ruby accused several of the husbands here of murdering Tessa's philandering husband, Andy Dejon because Andy had bedded their wives. Tessa and Ruby had driven around Abiquiu threatening to shoot the cuckolded husband who'd killed Andy. Fortunately none of the husbands turned out to be the murderer, so the sisters didn't have to shoot anyone. Nasty business, that.

As soon as he climbed out of the Cherokee Fernando noticed

the front door of the gallery ajar, as if someone had entered and not closed the door behind them. The open door surprised him, because he didn't see any vehicles parked in the adjoining lot. He walked over to the entrance and knocked on the half-opened door. No response. So he stepped inside and called out, "Tessa?" When no one responded, he eased into the dark gallery, seeing a few small counters and glass cabinets that had been smashed and looted, spilling much of their contents on the wooden floor. Glass and broken pieces of pottery, as well as pieces of jewelry, littered the floor. A pile of cheap Mexican rugs had been knocked over, blocking the hallway to Tessa's living quarters, a frame extension on the rear of the building.

"Tessa?" he called out again. Nothing. Only the sound of vehicles zipping by on the highway outside. Finally he gave up and walked back outside. He shut the door and made sure it locked behind him.

Turning, Fernando saw a young boy pedaling his bicycle alongside the highway. The kid surprised him by turning into the parking lot and coasting to a stop next to the Cherokee.

"Howdy," the kid said, a gangly freckle-face youngster with a lollipop sticking out of the corner of his mouth. Looked to be around ten or eleven. The kid pulled the lollipop out of his mouth and added, "She's not here."

"So I see," Fernando said, surprised by the kid's directness. "Do you happen to know where she is?"

"She always goes to stay at the hot springs when she's fighting with her husband, so probably Ojo Caliente," the kid said.

That gave Fernando pause. Did the kid know that Tessa's husband was dead? Should he tell the youngster?

"Lotta people here don't like her," the kid continued.

Fernando nodded. "I can see that. Do you know who spray-painted this graffiti and ransacked the gallery?"

"I gotta go," the kid said and turned his bike to go.

Fernando grabbed the handlebars. "What's your name?"

"Billy," the kid said. "Billy Snyder. I gotta go now, my pop's waiting for me at home. He doesn't like it when I talk to strangers. Especially here. He's one of them that don't like the missus."

Fernando released the handlebars and watched the kid peddle

away. The youngster glanced back at Fernando as he took off fast down the highway. The kid didn't look back again.

Puzzled, Fernando watched the kid disappear over a small rise. The kid, though at first forthcoming, seemed ill at ease talking to him. Why? After saying a lot of locals didn't like Tessa, the kid clammed up when asked if he knew who was responsible for the damage to Abiquiu Fine Art. The question seemed to frighten the youngster as if he were afraid of retribution if he answered.

Billy Snyder. Fernando took out his pocket notebook and scribbled down that name.

Now what? He decided to check out Ojo Caliente, the nearby hot springs. At least it wasn't Ghost Ranch. He'd stayed at Ojo a few times for a little rest and relaxation, back when he was working as a Santa Fe Police detective and needed some time off to chill. He liked the 100-year-old spa well enough. Ojo claimed to be one of the only hot springs on the planet that featured sulfur-free waters and four particular healing minerals: Arsenic, Lithia, Soda, and Iron. Whatever. He had no idea if any of that were true, only that lying around all day and soaking in one of their nine communal pools was definitely relaxing. At least for a day. After that it bored him to death. He'd often come up for the weekend and ended up wanting to leave after the first day. Estelle, on the other hand, always wanted to stay the full weekend. She claimed the hot springs were the one surefire antidote for her bad back. Finally they started bringing two cars. That way he could leave early and she could stay as long as she wanted.

The thing that irritated him most about the hot springs was listening to the New Agers who flocked there as if it were some sort of wellness Mecca, a fountain of youth. On his last visit to the spa he'd listened to this skinny, middle-aged woman spout off about how she came once a month to purge her body and mind, to wash off the negativity of the years, and to release the toxic experiences of her life. A ritual cleansing, she'd called it. He'd finally had enough and told her to shut up and leave him alone, which prompted Estelle to lecture him later about his rudeness. In his opinion it was the skinny woman who was being rude. Who wanted to listen to that crap? The toxic experiences of her life? Please!

No, he had zero tolerance for New Age bullshit. One of his many flaws, he supposed. Along with a propensity for being rude, according to Estelle and his daughters, who tended to agree with Estelle about his failures.

Cursing, Fernando climbed back into his Cherokee. Since Billy the kid said Tessa usually took refuge at Ojo Caliente after fights with her husband, it seemed likely she would do the same now, after one or more of the locals had attacked her gallery. Worth a try. Still, he wasn't thrilled at the prospect of driving all the way to Ojo Caliente since there was no direct route. He either had to backtrack to Española and take Highway 285 North, or take Highway 554 up to El Rito and then around to Highway 111. Highway 111 would take him down to Ojo. He for damned sure didn't want to go back to cluttered, unsightly Española, one of his least favorite cities, so he decided to take the longer route through El Rito.

Fernando drove back down the highway past the village of Abiquiu and then turned left on Highway 554. Once across the Chama River the countryside turned starkly beautiful, with distant gray, white, and pink mesas punctuated by the massive black rock formation of Sierra Negra Peak. Then it was a straight shot up past Alamosa Canyon to El Rito and then over to Highway 285. By the time he spotted the turn-off to Ojo Caliente the sun hung low in the western sky. Not a good sign. He still had to drive all the way back to Santa Fe.

He turned right and drove by the old Santa Cruz Church. Across the road stood the monstrous two story white house with the blue roof that he remembered from previous visits. The place looked like a reconditioned barn or military barracks. The bridge over dry Rio Ojo Caliente took him into the main parking lot. He parked near the original hotel, a 100-year-old building famous for its long veranda with arched stone colonnades. Several old timers sat in rocking chairs on the veranda watching him walk up to the front entrance. When he waved, one of the old bastards waved back. The others looked away.

Fernando grabbed the handrail and was about to climb the three steps up to the veranda when he changed his mind. Why alert the desk clerks that he was looking for Tessa Montez? This being a retreat where people came to get away, the staff probably wouldn't tell him anyway.

So instead he turned and walked through the elaborate desert gardens toward the bathhouses. He spotted bathers in the large communal hot pool, whereas the small private pools seemed deserted at this time of day. It was worth a try, he figured.

He entered the men's bathhouse quickly before any of the staff could see or question him. Inside, the damp steamy room smelled rank like a tired locker room or worse. Reminded him of the locker room at Santa Fe High back when he was sent against his will to Physical Education class, which he hated with a passion. Once inside, two young hipster types just coming out of the showers buck naked eyed him suspiciously as he walked across the slippery floor fully clothed and wearing heavy hiking boots. He turned away and stepped out of the door to the communal pool before they could say anything.

Outside Fernando found several bathers lounging in the large round pool, partially surrounded by a row of chaise lounge chairs. Walking toward the pool he heard a woman on a nearby chaise remark, "Hey cowboy, where's your trunks?"

He turned to find a middle-aged woman in a bikini and floppy white hat. She looked him over, from his jeans to his plaid shirt, licking her lips. "You looking for a good time?"

Fernando ignored the woman.

Moments later he spotted Tessa, who recognized him at about the same time. He waved.

Tessa smiled. She walked up the steps slowly, water flowing off her shapely body. Pausing, she shook the water from her long black hair. Then she came up out of the water like a Greek goddess.

Fernando couldn't take his eyes off her naked breasts and her tiny bikini bottom that failed to cover the tufts of pubic hair underneath. He saw why Blaine was so crazy about her. Tessa was drop-dead gorgeous, a younger and better-endowed version of her older sister Ruby.

When she reached the deck she again shook her head, flinging water left and right. "Fernando...what are you doing here?" she asked, reaching for a towel on her chaise.

"Ruby sent me," he replied. Not exactly true, but close enough, he figured. "That is, I need to talk to you about Sonny's shooting," he tried again, unable to take his eyes from her perfect body.

"Yeah? Well, let's go somewhere private," Tessa said. She dried herself with the towel and threw it around her shoulders.

Fernando followed her to the entrance of the women's bathhouse before realizing he couldn't enter.

Tessa pointed to the row of Pueblo Suites along the mesa hillside that ran behind the pools. "I'll meet you at my sweet, number forty-two." With that, she disappeared into the bathhouse.

Fernando walked back through the men's bathhouse, now empty except for a staff member mopping the slippery floor. The man stopped mopping when he saw Fernando and said, "Haven't you read the rules? You can't go into the pool area in street clothes. And no shoes allowed."

"Okay, I'll remember that," Fernando said, saluting.

Outside the bathhouse, Fernando walked around the pools to the hillside at the western edge of the hot springs. He spotted a trail that wound its way up the rocky slope. If he remembered correctly, the trail led to the ruins of Posi-Ouinge Pueblo, an ancestral Puebloan ruin that dated from the thirteenth century and once included some two thousand rooms. He'd hiked around the area one day many years ago when he'd come with Estelle and got tired of lounging around the pool. Not much up there, he remembered. Just a bunch of loose stones scattered about in the sand as if a giant hand had tossed them into the desert. Over the centuries all the walls had disintegrated into nothing. The destroyer of all things, time.

Lost in his reveries, Fernando didn't notice Tessa coming up behind him. "Hey-" she said, surprising him.

"Whoa, you surprised me," Fernando said, shaking his head, as though he were trying to wake up from a deep sleep. "I just came from Abiquiu and saw the damage to your gallery. "Do you know who did this?"

Tessa frowned, holding a large bath towel tight around her body. "I'm sure it's that fucking Ray Sandoval. Did Ruby tell you what happened? My cheating, ex-husband Andy got his wife pregnant. After Andy was murdered, Ray expected me to pay child support, if you can believe it. Lucky for me, Ruby hooked me up with her lawyer, Raoul Garcia, who told Ray to go fuck himself. After that Ray's been coming over to hassle me and sending me threatening texts."

Fernando noticed the purple bruise on the side of Tessa's face. He also noticed that Tessa's language was as colorful as Ruby's. "Did Sandoval give you that black eye?" he asked, remembering the thin, gangly man who managed the stables at Ghost Ranch who'd given them a hard time when they'd come to Abiquiu looking to find Andy's murderer. Fernando had accompanied Ruby and Tessa on what turned out to be a wild goose chase, just to keep them out of trouble. He'd succeeded at the time, but now it looked like Sandoval and his Abiquiu cohorts had turned on Tessa big time. Too much ill will in the village, starting with Andy and his carnal exploits and now continuing with Tessa accusing folks of murder.

Tessa nodded. "Yeah, he attacked me physically the day before yesterday at my gallery. Grabbed me and then smacked me a couple of times before I could get loose and kick the fucker in the nuts. That's why I came here...to get away," she said, beginning to walk toward the Pueblo Suites, which looked like attached adobe casitas built up against the rocky cliff of the mesa.

Fernando followed Tessa to Number forty-two. They walked through bright yellow chamisa bushes on either side of the entryway. Tessa opened the heavy wooden door and they stepped into a light, spacious room with a king size bed and a small sitting area containing a loveseat and stuffed chair. The casita came with a cozy kiva fireplace in one corner and heavy log vigas on the ceiling, adding to the Southwestern décor on the walls.

"Make yourself at home," Tessa said.

With that Tessa tossed her towel on the bed and walked back to the shower. Then she kicked out of her bikini bottom and tossed it on the bed with the towel. Now she stood buck naked in front of Fernando. "Give me a minute. I need to take a quick shower," she said, nonchalantly, as if standing nude in front of a stranger was as natural to her as taking a shower.

Fernando, on the other hand, was just tongue-tied and staring at the black pubic bush between Tessa's legs. Lush. That was the only word that popped into his mind. Lush!

Suddenly he felt the beginning of a monstrous erection in his jeans. He began to feel awkward, like a damn teenager again. He hadn't been in the presence of a naked, not to mention sexy, young woman in a very long time. In his sixties he still had a surprisingly strong libido, but this was neither the time nor the place to turn that bad boy loose.

What to do?

"Down boy," he told himself, trying to remember past strategies he'd used to control his erections. Think of the Pope. Think of your dear, saintly mother, Annie Lee McCarthy who met your father when they were both students at the University of New Mexico. Think of the many boring Santa Fe High School classes and teachers he had been forced to endure. Anything to avoid thinking of that bushy crevice between Tessa's legs.

"Are you okay?" Tessa asked, noticing that something was amiss. She stood buck naked next to the bed.

Too much.

"I'll be outside," Fernando stammered and stumbled out of the door trying to cover up the bulge in his jeans. Yes, like a damned teenager!

4

Fernando sat on a bench next to the flower garden, where trees and leafy red and yellow flowers provided cover. Cover from what? He felt foolish, having run from the sight of a beautiful naked woman. When he was younger he would have loved a peek at that, but now that he'd reached the ripe old age of sixty-five it seemed somehow inappropriate. Out of place. He couldn't remember the last time he'd gotten an erection while on the job, if what he was doing now qualified as a job. Good question. What exactly was he doing here?

Tessa joined him at the bench a few minutes later. Wearing tight white shorts and a low-cut blue blouse, she still looked drop dead sexy. But at least her private parts were covered, so Fernando could relax.

"There you are," she said, sitting down beside him. "So what did you want to talk to me about?"

"Have you heard about Sonny Davis?" Fernando asked.

Tessa shook her head. "Not really. Ruby left a garbled message on my phone this morning. Something about Sonny being shot. What happened?"

"Sonny was murdered in his gallery two days ago," Fernando said. "Turns out the murder weapon was Ruby's pistol, Jimmy Mackey's old Glock, which was found next to the body."

"Wait...you don't think Ruby killed Sonny, I hope," Tessa responded.

"I don't, no, but her fingerprints are all over the gun. Most likely yours too," Fernando said. "Manny brought Ruby in to the station as a suspect. He'll most likely bring you in next for fingerprinting and questioning. Maybe even as a suspect, I don't know."

Now Tessa looked worried. "But why would Ruby or I want to kill Sonny? That doesn't make any sense. Why would Manny suspect us? I mean, what motive would we have to kill him? He means nothing to us."

Fernando shrugged. "I don't know, maybe because the two of you had possession of the murder weapon and because Ruby hated and bad-mouthed Sonny to everyone every chance she got."

Tessa did not reply.

"What about the Glock?" Fernando asked. "Ruby said she hadn't seen the gun since the two of you went to Abiquiu to find your ex-husband's killer. That leaves you. Tell me if you know what happened to the gun, because, believe me, Manny won't ask nicely."

Tessa looked away. She didn't respond for a few moments. Then she said, "Okay... I took the gun to Blaine's gallery, after I decided to move in with him temporarily. I was paranoid after I started getting threats from Ray Sandoval. I wanted protection."

"Did anyone else have access to the gun?" Fernando asked. "Blaine must have known about it."

"Yeah, he was the one who put the gun away. He kept it in his desk drawer for safety, but I don't think he ever used it," Tessa said. "I mean, he has his own gun. I think it's also a Glock."

"Anyone else?"

Tessa shook her head. "No, because we kept it in his office. No one ever comes into the office except his drinking buddies from El Farol. You know the crowd. Ruby, Sonny, Dave Stein, June and Paul Bryan, and once in a while one of the other artists on Canyon Road."

"So one of them could have taken it," Fernando said, not a question.

Tessa shrugged.

"And you never noticed it was gone?" Fernando asked.

"No, because Blaine and I parted ways a few days ago, right after I found him with some floozy he picked up at La Fonda," Tessa said. "*In flagrante delicto.* I just told him to fuck off and grabbed my clothes and left. I don't need another philanderer like my ex-husband Andy. One of those assholes was enough."

"Really? Who was the bimbo?"

"Hah! I wasn't formally introduced!" Tessa replied. "She was a blond with big breasts, that's all I know."

Fernando nodded. "Well, anyway, you might want to go back to Santa Fe and stay with Ruby until all this sorts out. You'll find it's better to cooperate with Manny...to be as forthcoming as possible."

"Okay, I get it," Tessa shot back.

"What about this Ray Sandoval character?" Fernando asked, looking at her bruised face. "What are you going to do about him?"

"I filed a complaint," Tessa said. "The Rio Arriba County Sheriff is investigating, so I'm counting on them to take care of Sandoval. Early on I moved most of my gallery stock to a storage facility in Española. My insurance will cover what was damaged. Not a problem."

"Not a problem?" Fernando asked, taken aback by her cavalier attitude. She was about to be hauled in by the Santa Fe Police in connection with a murder investigation and at the same time was being threatened by an angry sociopath who had already vandalized her art gallery and attacked her physically. If she didn't have a problem, who did?

It took another half hour, but Fernando finally managed to convince Tessa to return to Santa Fe. First, though, she had to get more clothing and personal effects from her gallery in Abiquiu, so Fernando followed her back to the suite and watched her pack her suitcase.

After Teresa checked out, the two of them walked to the parking lot. Fernando placed her suitcase in the rear compartment of her white Honda CR-V and watched her drive off. Then he followed in his Cherokee, losing sight of her CR-V almost immediately. Tessa drove like her older sister Ruby—fast and furious, if not outright angry. On the other hand Fernando took it easy. Why rush? He knew precisely where they were headed.

By the time he reached Abiquiu it was nearly dark. Banks of crimson and purple clouds smothered the western horizon. Looked like rain was blowing in from the Pacific. He spotted Tessa's CR-V parked in front of Abiquiu Fine Art and the door to the gallery wide open. He pulled in behind the CR-V and walked into the gallery, looking as forlorn and ransacked as he remembered it. Lights were on in the living quarters, so he headed for the rear of the gallery. "Tessa?" he called out.

"Back here in the bedroom," she responded. "I'm getting my clothes together. Help yourself to a beer in the refrigerator, if you want."

Fernando needed no invitation. He made his way through the mess of broken glass and smashed furniture to the tiny efficiency kitchen in back, which included a two-burner stove and a mini refrigerator sitting on one of two countertops. The other countertop came with two cast-iron barstools. He opened the mini fridge and found a six pack of Coors, a spoiled half gallon of milk, a slab of moldy cheese, and a large container of yogurt. Looked like no one had cooked or eaten anything in this kitchen in a very long time. Disgusted, he reached into the mini fridge for a can of Coors and then slammed the door closed to block the rank smell.

Fernando sat on the nearest barstool and popped the top of the Coors. Not his favorite beer, but under the circumstances he couldn't very well complain. Too light, with not much taste.

Halfway through the beer he heard shuffling noises in the hallway. Was Tessa dragging a heavy suitcase outside to her CR-V? Then voices, followed by a slap and the sound of something crashing to the floor. "Hey!" Tessa shouted.

Instantly Fernando jumped up and hurried down the hall to the bedroom. Tessa lay on the floor sprawled on top of an open suitcase half filled with clothes. Over her stood none other than Ray Sandoval. The tall, thin Sandoval wore a leather vest over his Western shirt. Gesturing wildly with his hands and cursing Tessa, Sandoval turned when Fernando appeared in the doorway.

"You!" Sandoval spit.

"Leave her alone," Fernando said.

"Who do you think you are," Sandoval shot back. "I owe you from the last time we met. Maybe it's time I teach you a lesson."

Sandoval left Tess and approached Fernando, his firsts balled.

Fernando waited. At 5-10 and 180 pounds of muscle from thirty years of police work, he wasn't worried about Sandoval, who looked like a damned scarecrow without the stuffing. A strong wind would blow him away.

Sandoval didn't waste any time. He shoved Fernando back away from the door and then launched a right uppercut that caught Fernando under the chin and sent him falling backwards on his ass.

Fernando sat still for several seconds, smiling at Sandoval.

Scarecrow man had more pop than he expected, but not nearly enough. Then he got to his feet and moved toward Sandoval, who lashed out with a straight right hand.

Fernando blocked the punch with his left hand and stepped forward. With all his 180 pounds, he drove his right hand hard into Sandoval's gut. A technique he'd learned years ago that never failed.

Sandoval groaned and bent over clutching his midsection. That's when Fernando finished his business. He brought his knee up quickly and smashed it into Sandoval's face, which sent Sandoval reeling backwards, his nose spurting blood. He collapsed on the floor and then tried to crawl away on his hands and knees.

"What's a matter, I thought you were a tough guy—or is that only when you're beating up women?" Fernando taunted the fallen man. "You touch Tessa again and she'll be the last woman you ever touch." With that he kicked Sandoval in the ass and sent him crashing into the wall of the hallway. He followed Sandoval into the front of the gallery, kicking him along, and watched him get to his feet and stagger outside to his truck. The bloodied Sandoval managed to open the door and plop down in the driver's seat of the truck.

Fernando stood in the doorway of the gallery and watched Sandoval sitting in the driver's seat of his pickup trying to stop his nosebleed with a handkerchief. Finally Sandoval tossed aside his handkerchief and started the engine and then eased out on the highway.

Fernando watched until the pickup disappeared around the curve leading to Ghost Ranch. Good riddance, he said to himself. But he knew Sandoval would likely be back. If so, he would finish it once and for all.

Walking into the gallery, he found Tessa in the bedroom closing her suitcase. She didn't have any new injuries, as far as he could see.

"Is he gone?" she asked.

Fernando nodded. "Are you okay?"

"Yeah, he just slapped at me while I was trying to move away, which made me loose my balance," Tessa said. "I didn't hurt anything when I fell."

"Good," Fernando said, looking at a pile of clothes on the bed that would in no way fit into her already overstuffed suitcase. "What about the rest of the clothes? Do you have another suitcase?"

"No, just this one suitcase," Tessa said. "That should last me for another week or so. I can come back and get more when things get settled. I think I will go back to Ruby's, at least for a while."

Fernando carried the suitcase outside and placed it in the rear compartment of her CR-V while Tessa locked the gallery.

"Thanks," Tessa said before getting into the CR-V.

"No problem," Fernando said. "He won't bother you again. If he does, let me know and I'll finish it."

Tessa looked at him funny, not knowing what he meant.

He didn't know either.

5

Fernando slept late next morning. Rough night. By the time he'd followed Tessa back to Santa Fe yesterday evening and helped her carry her suitcase into Ruby's gallery it was past nine o'clock. His wife Estelle was pissed when he finally made it home because he hadn't called to tell her he would be late, as per their agreement. She'd left his dinner on a plate in the microwave, a couple of chicken tacos and some posole, served with a green chile salsa.

"You know how to operate the microwave, right...even though you apparently don't know how to operate your cell phone," Estelle said, sarcastically. "I'm off to bed. I have an early day tomorrow at the church."

So he was in the doghouse this morning. Once again. He took a long hot shower and dressed quickly in jeans and a blue work shirt, careful to avoid the mirror. Superstitious, he believed that he aged every time he looked in the mirror. Every time he glanced at his salt and pepper hair, he saw more salt than pepper. Don't look, don't age, that was the trick.

For breakfast Fernando made himself a quick omelet with cheese and green chile and then took it outside to his bench on their patio, along with a cup of coffee from the pot Estelle had left. He liked to be outside as much as possible in these last dying days of summer. Autumn was coming on fast now—soon the temps would dip below his comfort level and he would have to dress for the cold weather, which he dreaded. The cold seemed to stiffen his joints a little more every year.

When he finished his omelet, he carried the plate back into the kitchen and poured himself another cup of coffee. He drank at least three cups of coffee every morning and needed every last bit of the caffeine. Back outside, he sat on his bench looking out on the big cottonwoods that protected their property from the neighbors, all new imports from the east or west costs, rich people who could afford to buy million dollar homes. The over-class.

While he drank his second cup of coffee he reviewed yesterday's events. He worried that both Ruby and Tessa could be in big trouble. Both of them handled the Glock that killed Sonny Davis and both had a widely-shared motive to kill Sonny: that he was a violent, woman-beater who needed to be stopped. And neither had an alibi that would stand up in court.

The good news for Ruby and Tessa was that there were several other sets of fingerprints on the murder weapon. Blaine's, for sure, since he'd stored the Glock in his desk after Tessa brought it to his gallery, at least according to Tessa. No doubt some of the other fingerprints belonged to Blaine's artist friends and drinking buddies on Canyon Road. That would include Sonny himself, Dave Stein, June and Paul Bryan, and maybe a couple of the other artists on Canyon Road who occasionally showed up at El Farol for happy hour.

The bad news was that the list of other possible suspects didn't sound all that promising. Sonny couldn't very well shoot himself in the back multiple times. Dave Stein was so old he could barely walk, let alone carry out a killing. The Bryans were much too stiff and squeaky clean to be taken seriously as murderers. That left Ruby and Tessa as the most likely suspects, unless someone else turned up.

What about Blaine? Fernando had to wonder. He allowed Tessa to bring the gun to his gallery; even kept the gun in his desk. On the other hand, Blaine had no obvious motive, since Sonny was one of his drinking buddies. And let's face it, Blaine's reputation with women wasn't much better than Sonny's. Blaine might not be a woman-beater, but he for damn sure wasn't any Sir Galahad either.

Tired of brooding, Fernando went for a walk along Acequia Madre Street. He'd been trying to walk every day, his one and only concession to Estelle who wanted him to exercise more. Once he got outside and started walking he actually enjoyed the exercise and the mild, sunny day so typical of Santa Fe this time of year. So much so that when he returned he decided to do some yard work. Estelle had been after him for the last week to trim the dead stalks on their hollyhocks. She wouldn't let him touch her roses. Only Estelle was allowed to tend her rose garden.

He found his rake and pruning shears in their garage and went to work. When finished, he bagged the cuttings and threw the bag into their waste bin. By then it was time for lunch, so he cleaned up inside and heated up a bowl of green chile stew in the microwave. He didn't like to eat big breakfasts or lunches. He saved his big meal for dinner when he and Estelle could eat together, as they had done for the past thirty-some years.

After lunch Fernando went back outside with another cup of coffee to relax. He'd just finished his coffee when he heard a car coming down Acequia Madre. The car surprised him by turning into his driveway, a powder blue Mercedes coupe that looked as out of place here as a damned UFO landing. Who in the hell would drive a powder blue Mercedes in Santa Fe? And why would anyone ridiculous enough to drive a powder blue Mercedes come to see him?

The Mercedes eased up behind his Cherokee and sat idling for a few seconds before the engine switched off. Then the driver sat in the Mercedes for several long minutes, apparently staring at Fernando out of the dark windows. Did the driver want Fernando to walk over to greet him or what? Well, Fernando had some news for powder blue: go fuck yourself.

Finally Fernando saw a heavy-set, fire-plug of a man climb awkwardly out of the Mercedes. He frowned, recognizing the one and only Raoul Garcia step out of the Mercedes. Here comes trouble. A sometime friend, sometime enemy, Raoul had the reputation of being the best criminal lawyer in the state of New Mexico, the kind of lawyer who could get off the guiltiest of the guilty. Raoul brushed the wrinkles out of his dark blue suit and then straightened his sunglasses. Looking dangerously bloated, with gray hair slicked back on his balding head, Raoul spotted Fernando on the patio and waved with a flip of his wrist.

Raoul was no longer the fiery young lawyer Fernando remembered from their youth. Back then Raoul represented radical Chicano leaders and organizations like La Raza as far back as the late seventies. He called his clients "political prisoners," men and women charged with everything from growing pot to making armed raids on county courthouses. Raoul built a reputation for taking on the system every chance he got and winning more times than he lost.

Not an easy task for an aggressive, smart-ass Chicano lawyer who all the Anglos in the judicial system hated. But times had changed, and so had Raoul and his clientele. Instead of fire-bombing courthouses, the young apolitical hoodlums he represented now shot each other in gangs over territory or drugs. If not for territory or drugs, then just for the hell of it. And Raoul had changed along with the times. He now did a lucrative business in real estate development and celebrity lawsuits, having become one of the premier trial lawyers in all of northern New Mexico. There wasn't a lawyer or district attorney in the state who didn't fear coming up against Raoul in a courtroom. And for good reason.

"So it's true, then. You took down your shingle," Raoul said, lumbering up to the patio. He looked stiff and barely ambulatory, as if he were suffering from some joint disease, maybe just bad arthritis.

"Yep, I retired. Now I just take an occasional job cleaning up other people's messes," Fernando said.

Raoul laughed. "Cleaning up other people's messes? That'll keep you in business forever, amigo. People are damned good at creating messes and not so good at cleaning them up. Provides a lotta business for people like you and me."

"What brings you to these parts?" Fernando asked, cutting short the chit-chat. He walked across the patio to meet the big man, whose breathing appeared to be labored. With a bulging belly and fingers the size of sausages, Raoul bore no resemblance to the fiery young radical of the bad old days. In fact, he looked like a candidate for a massive heart attack.

"Jesus, Raoul, are you okay?" Fernando asked, seriously worried about his old friend/enemy. "You look like death warmed over."

"Tell me about it," Raoul said. "It's my fucking heart. Too many widow makers for breakfast and margaritas for dinner. Doc says I need bypass heart surgery immediately or I'll be dead within the year, but I don't trust those greedy motherfuckers. I'm almost seventy, so what's the point? Life is a one-way ticket, my friend."

With that, Raoul reached out a meaty hand, his fingers covered with garish rings. Then he pumped Fernando's hand a little too forcefully.

"Have a seat," Fernando said.

Raoul sat in a wooden patio chair across from Fernando's bench. He looked around the yard. "Not bad, not bad at all. I see you've kept the original look of the house. Fuck the neighbors."

Fernando laughed. "You of all people should approve of that."

"Oh, I do," Raoul replied.

"So what's up?"

"Your friends, that's what's up," Raoul said. "Ruby and her sister and that crazy fucker Blaine Rogers. All three of them showed up at my office today hysterical as a bunch of hyenas. Turns out their fingerprints are all over the gun that killed Sonny Davis and they want me to keep their asses out of jail. Ruby said I should talk to you—that you would know who really killed Sonny. Do you?"

Fernando laughed. "No idea."

Raoul slapped his hands on his legs. "I didn't think so."

"Have you talked to Manny?" Fernando asked.

Raoul made a face. "Yeah, I talked to Manny. He's a silly bastard, with all his joking. I get tired of listening to him. He's not half the cop you were back in the day, that's for sure."

"He's maturing—slowly," Fernando said, thinking he should defend Manny although he basically agreed with Raoul's assessment of Manny.

"Very slowly!" Raoul said, laughing. "He did provide some useful information, though. Turns out everybody's fingerprints are on that fucking gun: Ruby, Tessa, Blaine, Sonny, the three bimbos who work for Sonny, and a few yahoos they haven't even identified. Half the fucking city of Santa Fe must have been playing with that gun. That's the first thing."

Fernando nodded. "That doesn't surprise me, because half the city of Santa Fe hated Sonny's guts."

"Second, the door to Athena Gallery wasn't damaged," Raoul continued. "That means either the shooter had a key or Sonny left the door unlocked. Probably the latter, because Sonny didn't even have his security system working, which means there's no video. Sonny was one careless motherfucker. No surprise, given the way he lived and the risks he took with his bimbos."

"He was screwing all three of them," Fernando added.

"I know, that's what I'm talking about," Raoul said. "All of which means that Ruby and the gang have nothing to worry about. Too many contingencies—too many ifs, ands and buts. Too many people with motives and not enough hard evidence to convict any one of them. Manny's smart enough to know that. No prosecutor would touch this case, unless something big turns up. Especially since everyone in town knows what a piece of shit Sonny was. How you gonna impanel an impartial jury who would give a damn about Sonny Davis."

"Better off dead."

"Exactly... that's the general opinion of Sonny," Raoul added. "You can't blame them, given Sonny's track record. What about you? What's your involvement in all this, Lopez? Ruby seems to think you're on the case."

Fernando laughed, shaking his head.

"Well, are you on the goddamn case or not, amigo?" Raoul asked, looking at Fernando suspiciously, as if he thought Fernando was being coy or withholding information.

Fernando did not respond. To tell the truth, he didn't know if he was on the case or not.

"I'll tell you what...if you find out who shot Sonny, call me right away," Raoul said. "Don't tell anyone else. Just keep it between you and me, okay? I'll make it worth your while. Couple thousand, maybe more. What do you say?"

Again Fernando said nothing. He had never considered and had no intention of ever working for Raoul. But let the big man talk. He would at least listen.

Raoul smiled. "Who knows, maybe we could be a team. Kinda like Perry Mason and what's his name, the investigator. You're the best goddamn detective this town has ever seen, and I'm the best goddamn lawyer. So why not?"

"We'll see," Fernando said finally. "This one's gonna be tough. Too many people involved. Murky."

Raoul smiled. "True, lotta people wanted that motherfucker dead, but only a limited number had access to that gun. Follow the gun."

With that, Raoul stood up stiffly and massaged his back. "Getting old sucks, but what's the alternative?"

Fernando watched Raoul hobble back to his Mercedes, still rubbing his back. Raoul climbed into the powder blue Mercedes and hit the ignition. Honking, he drove off down the driveway and turned left on Acequia Madre heading for the Paseo.

After Raoul left, Fernando lingered on the patio thinking about what Raoul had said. Follow the gun.

The Glock that killed Sony Davis traveled from Ruby's gallery to Blaine's gallery and then on to Sonny's gallery. The gun stopped at Athena Gallery. Maybe that was the key.

Besides Sonny, who was dead, Fernando knew there were at least three people who worked at Athena Gallery full-time: the three young bimbos Sonny hired to work there and service his sexual needs. He'd seen their smiles the day he'd forced Sonny to sign the divorce papers that ended his marriage to Athena Loering. They loved seeing someone get the best of Sonny. The three bimbos. Maybe that was the place to start his investigation, if that's what this was—an investigation.

Tired of brooding, Fernando checked the time and realized Happy Hour was about to begin at El Farol. Precisely what he needed on another exasperating day of too many questions and too few answers.

6

Fernando parked in the lot across the street from El Farol. He locked the Cherokee and walked across Canyon Road to the venerable El Farol, one of the many historic buildings on Canyon Road. The restaurant/bar dated from 1835 and was still going strong, hosting a variety of flamenco and other musical events. It was a great place to drink or eat, as everyone on Canyon Road could testify, especially the artistic types who usually skipped the eating.

He stepped up on the long porch where two young people were already sitting at one of the outdoor tables with a bottle of wine between them. Sitting close, they seemed to be celebrating some occasion, raising glasses of red wine in a toast of some sort and whispering to each other. Above them a string of lights and red chile ristras hung from the ceiling of the porch, its beams and railings and windows painted a chocolate brown color that contrasted with the tan stucco on the adobe. After a recent remodel, the place looked like a million bucks.

Fernando walked into the noisy bar, already crowded with celebrants. Most everyone who came to El Farol was a regular, which was why the artists on Canyon Road loved it. They didn't take kindly to the presence of tourists, most of them toting camera equipment, who insisted on taking photographs of everyone and everything. Very irritating. He spotted Ruby back in the restaurant part of El Farol, sitting at a table in front of a flashy colored mural of musicians and flamenco dancers. Ruby sat next to Dave Stein, a wizened little man in his eighties with olive skin that glowed and wisps of gray hair sticking up from various parts of his skull and out of his big ears. Dave wore the same blue suit that he'd worn for a decade.

Across from the two of them sat Blaine and Tessa, a picture of summer. Blaine wore his standard red Bermuda shorts with a turquoise Hawaiian shirt, while Tessa wore a skimpy red tank top with black tights. Complicating the picture, the two of them seemed to be arguing. Looked like Tessa was giving Blaine a scolding, while Blaine sat there shaking his head, denying everything or asking forgiveness, whatever. Someone else sat at the table with her back to Fernando, an elderly woman with gray curly hair wearing an expensive tailored suit, something you didn't often see during Happy Hour at El Farol.

"Fernando, come join us," Ruby called from across the room.

Fernando bought a Modelo draft at the bar and then walked over to the table. Ruby looked her gallery-owner finest today, with a low-cut silk blouse the color of wine and black slacks. "You look gorgeous, Ruby," he said, pulling up a chair.

"Fernando!" the elderly woman greeted him.

Instantly he recognized Athena Loering, the ex-wife of Sonny Davis and former owner of Athena Gallery. He hadn't seen her since she returned to her wealthy family in Cincinnati after Sonny signed their divorce papers, giving him Athena Gallery but nothing else, thanks to Fernando. By signing Sonny had forfeited any claim on Athena's wealth. Athena had paid Fernando $25,000 to make Sonny an offer he couldn't refuse. Fernando's Smith & Wesson had sealed the deal.

"Athena...what a surprise to see you here," Fernando said. "I thought you were in Cincinnati."

"I was, until I heard about Sonny," Athena replied. "I had to come back to deal with Athena Gallery. I'm taking care of the day-to-day affairs while trying to sell the gallery. I brought my brother Tom with me to help."

"Wait until you hear this," Ruby interjected. "Athena didn't give Sonny the gallery outright, she gave him a controlling fifty-five percent. She kept the other forty-five percent in case something like this happened. Now she has one hundred percent. That's one smart woman."

Fernando shook his head. He didn't know exactly what to say. Was Athena celebrating or mourning? "Well, I'm sorry for your loss," he said finally, choosing the latter.

"Don't be," Athena said. "He was a no-good drunk and soccer hooligan who liked to beat up women. He got what he deserved. I have no pity for him, as terrible as that sounds."

"Perfectly understandable," Ruby said.

Fernando sat next to Athena and took a long drink of his Modelo, at a loss for words. Everybody and their uncle hated Sonny. Was it any surprise that Sonny was murdered? Maybe the real mystery was why it took so long for someone to finally pull the trigger.

"That's the good news, Athena's back," Ruby said. "The bad news is that Manny's trying to pin Sonny's murder on one of us because of my goddamn gun, which Tessa stupidly took to Blaine's gallery and Blaine stupidly took to Athena Gallery."

Confused, Fernando said, "Wait. What did you say? Blaine took the gun to Athena Gallery?"

"Yes...didn't you know that? I thought you were looking into the murder for me?" Ruby said to Fernando.

Fernando threw up his hands. Then he turned to Blaine. "Why did you take the gun to Athena Gallery?"

"To keep it away from Tessa," Blaine blurted out. "Look at her—she has a hot temper, I thought she might use it on me after my one indiscretion with the skank I met at La Fonda. So I gave it to Sonny and told him to lock it up somewhere safe or throw the damn thing away."

"Whatever!" Ruby shouted, drawing the bartender's attention. The bartender shook his head, not wanting to deal with another scene created by Ruby and Blaine, who were notorious for getting thrown out of El Farol.

"If Tessa hadn't taken the gun, none of this would have happened," Ruby continued. "It's as simple as that."

"Don't! Don't start on me!" Tessa yelled at Ruby, Tessa's eyes were bright red, as though she'd been crying.

"It's okay, nobody's blaming you, just forget Ruby," Blaine said, stroking Tessa's arm.

Tessa shot up in her chair. "Get your hands off me, you bastard! Why'd you have to go fuck that woman at La Fonda? Just leave me alone!"

With that Tessa turned violently and stomped off toward the door, knocking over her chair.

Now Blaine stood up and yelled, "I'm sorry! It meant nothing to me! Can't you understand? Nothing!"

"That's great, Blaine. It meant nothing. That makes it so much better! Go fuck yourself!" Tessa replied and walked out the door, raising her right hand high over her head with the middle finder extended.

Absolutely everyone in El Farol was staring at them now. The bartender opened his arms wide, as if asking 'what the fuck?'.

Blaine shrugged. He sat down and drained his margarita. Then he raised his glass and asked for another. The bartender frowned and shook his head skeptically but went to work mixing another margarita.

Athena turned to Fernando. "I see you guys haven't changed."

Fernando laughed. "No, we haven't. Or they haven't anyway."

"Thanks again for helping persuade Sonny to sign the divorce papers," Athena said. "I never got a chance to thank you properly."

Fernando raised his hand. "No need. I was glad to help. He was a piece of work, for sure."

Meanwhile Blaine and Ruby began arguing about which one of them was to blame for Tessa's outburst, Ruby for saying Tessa was responsible for moving Ruby's gun, or Blaine for fucking the woman at La Fonda, whose name Blaine couldn't remember. Jessica maybe or maybe not. Finally the bartender left his station and came over to tell the bickering couple to lower their voices or take it outside. In response, Ruby and Blaine continued bickering, but in quieter tones.

"What are you going to do with the gallery now?" Fernando asked. "Are you thinking about coming back to run it?"

Athena shook her head. "I don't think so. I'll probably sell both it and my house in Hyde Park Estates, but I want to spend some time in Santa Fe, just to see if I might want to move back at some point."

Fernando nodded. "By the way, how'd you find out about Sonny?"

Instantly Athena looked perplexed, confused. "Oh, well, I guess it must have been one of the girls, maybe Mary Margaret. And then the police called, I can't remember the man's name...."

Why the confusion? It was a simple question. Fernando didn't know what to make of her response.

"I came as soon as I could, you know, to clean up the mess," Athena continued. "I had no idea the police hadn't arrested the murderer. I thought it would be a simple matter of tracing the gun, but I guess not."

"Too many suspects," Fernando said. "Too many people who had access to the gun."

"So I gather...." Athena finished her glass of wine and gathered her purse. "Well, I need to be on my way. I'm staying at La Fonda until we can open my house in Hyde Park Estates. If you need to get a hold of me, call my cell phone or leave a message at the front desk at La Fonda. Are you still working as a private eye?"

"Retired," Fernando said. "Although, if the need arises, I sometimes take a case as a fixer."

"Fixer?"

"Yeah, like your case. Getting Sonny to sign the divorce agreement," Fernando said. "A fixer."

Athena smiled. "Well, then, I might be in touch." She stood up from the table and walked out of El Farol without looking back.

Blaine and Ruby were still bickering when Fernando finished his Modelo and left El Farol. He walked across Canyon Road to the parking lot and then stopped and reconsidered. Maybe he should check on Tessa, who seemed distraught when she more or less ran out of El Farol. So he walked up Canyon Road to Ruby's gallery, seeing his former office off to the side of the gallery. The office had remained empty, Ruby keeping it open just in case he changed his mind and wanted to resume his private eye business. Not likely.

Coming closer he spotted Tessa throwing loose clothing into the rear of her CR-V. He walked up behind her, noticing her suitcase and a few other odds and ends already in the compartment. She turned around ferociously and snapped, "I'm leaving—fuck all of you!"

Fernando stopped in his tracks. "Hey, don't include me. I didn't accuse you of anything."

Tessa eyed him suspiciously. "Then what do you want?"

"I just wanted to know if you were all right," Fernando said. "Where are you going?"

"You know where I'm going," Tessa replied.

Fernando nodded. He took a business card out of his wallet and handed it to Tessa. "Here, take this. If you need help, just give me a call. I closed my office, but my cell phone number is still the same."

Tessa looked at the card and then smiled. "Thanks, I might do that."

Fernando stood back as Tessa closed the rear door of the CR-V and climbed into the driver's seat. He watched her drive off down Canyon Road. She stuck her arm out of the window. Instead of giving him the finger, she actually waved.

7

Fernando tossed and turned all night thinking about Ruby's Glock changing hands from one person to another, one gallery to another. It was Tessa who moved the gun from Ruby's gallery to Blaine's Picasso and Company, and Blaine who moved the gun from Picasso and Company to Sonny's Athena Gallery, the end of the line. So Sonny turned out to be the key, the keeper of the gun. That meant all of Sonny's employees—Mary Margaret, Angelica, and Becca—would have had access to the gun, as well as Sonny's friends and drinking buddies at El Farol. Sonny was a sloppy drunk, a careless man who may very well have left the gun lying on his desk, where anyone could have picked it up and used it. Including his killer.

Tired of rehashing all this, Fernando finally said the hell with it and climbed out of bed. Estelle had already left for work. She'd become a workaholic since he'd retired, working long hours for the Immigrant Outreach Program at the church. He couldn't complain because he had been an absent husband for most of the thirty years he'd worked at the Santa Fe Police Department. He knew Estelle enjoyed the work and that the work was important, but he still missed her in the mornings. Now he knew how she'd felt all those years.

Not one to linger in the shower, he took an exceptionally long one this morning, hoping the hot water would wake him up. It didn't. So he dressed slowly and shuffled clumsily down the hall to the kitchen. Estelle had left a note on the table saying she would be late for dinner tonight and he would have to fend for himself. That made him feel even more lonesome. Downright abandoned.

Fernando brewed himself a cup of coffee in his Keurig and sat down at the kitchen table. He couldn't bear to eat anything this morning. Maybe he could find a pastry or something in their old-fashioned tin breadbox that Estelle insisted on keeping even though the tin had rusted in multiple spots. The breadbox had been a wedding present forty years ago.

Sure enough, he found a days old croissant hard as a rock. He softened the pastry by putting it in the microwave for fifteen seconds and then took it and his coffee outside to the patio. After his first cup of coffee his mind began to clear. After the second cup he'd come to a decision. This morning he would go down to Athena Gallery and see what he could learn from Sonny's employees, the three young women Sonny hired to run the gallery and also to administer to his carnal needs. He hadn't been to the gallery since he'd coerced Sonny into signing Athena's divorce papers and picked up a nice fat check from Athena.

He wanted to avoid Athena, if possible. She'd seemed so nervous, so flustered when he asked how she'd heard of Sonny's murder. The question required only a simple answer, so why did it distress her?

Fernando waited until ten o'clock, when he knew the gallery would be open. Then he drove down Acequia Madre to the Paseo and around to Canyon Road. By habit he parked in the lot between Ruby's gallery and Essentia, the sex shop owned by June and Paul Bryan, and then walked down Canyon Road to Athena Gallery, which sat back from Canyon Road about fifty feet. The sculpture garden in front drew him to the front door, through a walkway of Greek and Roman themed marble statues mixed with a few Native American bronzes. The surrounding plantings and flower gardens were so immaculately tended they looked English. The gallery screamed money, even before you entered the building with its pale beige stucco that seemed to radiate light and its front door painted bright blue to supposedly ward off evil spirits, according to local lore, which was just that: lore.

Fernando opened the door and stepped inside a glowing palace of color. Huge oil paintings hung from the walls in meticulous arrangement, with each painting given enough space to make it stand out individually. Huge paintings, as large as area rugs: five by seven, six by eight, and two enormous red paintings that took up the entire rear wall. All modernist abstracts that could have been on loan from a major gallery. Walking through the front room Fernando didn't see a single painting for sale under five digits. It was clear to him that Athena Gallery catered to a very small crowd: the filthy rich, whether they be tourists or local Santa Feans.

He saw two women in the gallery, both young, blond, thin, and dressed as if they were on their way to the Oscars' Red Carpet, even if they were more likely to end up on Sonny's bed than any red carpet. He recognized the older of the two from his last visit when he strong-armed Sonny and made him sign the divorce agreement. The woman smiled and came over to greet him.

"Well, hello, Mr. Lopez," the woman said, a tall blonde with a short, pixie hairdo. "I remember you from last time. You created quite a scene."

Fernando laughed. "You didn't seem to mind. I saw the smile on your face. You and your colleague over there."

Now the woman laughed with Fernando. "My name's Mary Margaret. I'm the store manager now, at least until Athena sells the gallery. I don't know if you've heard, but she's back in town

"I do, I talked to her yesterday at El Farol."

"We're kind of in limbo at the moment," Mary Margaret added. "Waiting to see what happens."

Fernando nodded. "I wanted to ask you about the pistol that killed Sonny. Apparently, Blaine Rogers, the owner of Picasso and Company, brought the gun here and gave it to Sonny for safe-keeping. Do you remember seeing it here?"

"Yes, the gun was on Sonny's desk, let me show you," she said, leading the way into what had been Sonny's office, decked out with a large antique mahogany desk and a full-service bar along the rear wall. A Taos sofa with rumpled blankets took up most of a side wall. Knowing Sonny and his appetites, it wasn't hard to guess the purpose of the Taos sofa.

Mary Margaret pointed to a shelf on the top of the desk. "The gun was right here on this shelf. Funny, though, it disappeared on the day Sonny was murdered. Someone must have taken it."

'That was my next question," Fernando responded. "Who all had access to the gun?"

"Really, anyone who walked into his office could have picked it up," Mary Margaret said.

"Like who?"

"Well, the three of us who work here, for starters," Mary Margaret said. "Angelica, Becca, and of course me, but I didn't come near it because I've always hated guns."

"Anybody else?" Fernando asked.

"Sure, like I said, anyone who walked into the office," Mary Margaret said. "Could have been Blaine or one of the artists that Sonny shows here, they stop by from time to time to check on sales. I can't think of anybody in particular. Sonny didn't have many good friends other than the El Farol crowd."

"I wonder why?" Fernando said sarcastically.

Mary Margaret smiled.

"So who's the woman over by the counter?"

"That's Angelica. Becca's not here today. It might be her day off, I'm not sure," Mary Margaret said.

Fernando walked across the room to the counter, where a younger woman stood idly by, looking like a manikin. With shoulder length blond hair and red lipstick, she bore an unmistakable resemblance to Taylor Swift. Probably intentional, since everyone under thirty seemed to be obsessed with Taylor Swift. They even called themselves Swifties. Was Angelica a Swifty?

"I'm not sure we've met," Fernando said.

"Oh yes, I saw what you did to Sonny," she said cheerfully, almost joyfully, a big smile on her face.

"You probably heard me talking to Mary Margaret," Fernando said. "I'm trying to trace the pistol that killed Sonny. Blaine Rogers gave it to Sonny for safe-keeping. Did you see the gun on Sonny's desk?"

Angelica nodded. "Yes."

"Did you ever see anyone handle the gun? Sonny or anyone else?" Fernando asked.

She hesitated a moment. "Well, the day before he was murdered, Sonny called me into his office at closing time. After we finished, he grabbed the gun and started waving it around, saying he was going to use it to shoot his ex-wife."

"Finished what?" Fernando asked.

Angelica blushed.

Fernando quickly realized it was better not to pursue what Angelica and Sonny were doing in his office, so to change the subject he asked, "And why would he want to shoot his ex-wife? I mean, they were divorced. She'd given him the gallery and moved back to Cincinnati. Why would he shoot her?"

"Because he found out she still owned part of the gallery," Angelica said. "Sonny wanted to sell the gallery quickly and go back to England. He said he was tired of the States. He didn't care how much he sold the gallery for, he just wanted to get ride of it fast."

"Tired of the States," Fernando said, amused. No more tired of the States than the States were tired of him.

"Something about football," Angelica said. "I mean soccer."

"Interesting, very interesting," Fernando said, nodding. "So they were fighting over which one of them would sell the gallery. Now Athena gets to sell the gallery and doesn't have to split the proceeds."

Angelica did not respond.

Fernando turned away and then stopped. "By the way, what do you get out of this arrangement?" He pointed to the Taos sofa in the office.

Angelica blushed again. "Sonny pays us well, two or three times what we'd make at any other gallery," she said. "And Sonny's not so bad, really. He's like a bad little boy who's experienced past trauma of some sort. Kind of sad, if you want to know the truth. A sad little boy. That's what I think, anyway."

Fernando bit his tongue. He could think of a few choice words to describe Sonny—a sad little boy would not be among them. "Okay, here's my card," he said finally, handing Angelica his card. "My cell phone number is on the card if you think of anything else."

With that, Fernando walked out of the gallery and paused to watch the tourists walk by on Canyon Road. Not even Noon and already the street was jammed with tourists carrying their cameras and shopping bags. Life in a tourist town. The price of living in paradise.

He walked up to Ruby's parking lot and headed for his Cherokee. Halfway there he changed his mind and instead went into Ruby's gallery. Stepping inside, he found Ruby brewing a cup of coffee in the little room she'd remodeled as a lunch room. Ruby looked bedraggled this morning, her hair sticking out every which way and wearing old shorts and a T-shirt. Looked like she'd just gotten out of bed. Strange since she'd already opened the gallery.

"Good morning," Fernando said. "Rough night?"

Ruby gave him the Evil Eye as only Ruby could. "Rough morning. I got a call from Tessa. The fuckers keep spray-painting her gallery in Abiquiu with nasty slogans. There were more today."

"Which fuckers?" Fernando asked. "You mean Ray Sandoval?"

"I guess," Ruby said. "The same ones who have been harassing her. Sandoval is one of them."

Fernando shook his head. "Jesus! What's Tessa gonna do?"

"Well, she can't stay in Abiquiu, that's for damn sure," Ruby said, sighing. "I've told her to bring all her stuff down here. If she gets tired of Blaine, she can share my gallery. It's plenty big. Plus, I have the pottery co-op. She could bring some of her stock down there. Maybe she'll listen now. I don't think it's safe for her to stay in Abiquiu. Not after this."

Fernando quickly tried to think of a way to help. Then it occurred to him. "I can go up and help—see what I can do for her. I know where she's staying." As soon as the words left his mouth, Fernando began to question his motives. Was it really to help Tessa? Or was it for more personal reasons? After all, Tessa was a very attractive young woman, as he could verify after seeing her *au naturel*. He couldn't decide. Both maybe. Or so he told himself.

Ruby cracked a smile. She came over and gave Fernando a hug. "Thanks, you're the best. Tessa can use all the help she can get. As for me, I need to get cleaned up fast. I look like something the dog dragged in."

"Yes, you do," Fernando said.

Ruby gave him the Evil Eye. Again. "You don't have to agree!"

8

O n the way out of town Fernando stopped at his house on Acequia Madre to pick up his Smith & Wesson. He locked the pistol, holster and all, in his glove compartment and drove around the Paseo to the entrance of Highway 84/285. From there he followed the usual route past the Santa Fe Opera and the turn-off to Tesuque, slowing down when he entered the Pojoaque commercial strip. Past the old Line Camp building he sped up again, heading into Española. When he saw a Lotaburger on the strip, he decided to stop for a quick lunch. He turned off the highway into the drive-thru and ordered a cheeseburger with green chile and coffee, his usual. To save time he parked and ate the cheeseburger sitting in the Cherokee.

When finished, Fernando pulled out on the highway and turned left on Highway 84. He loved this road, which followed the Chama River into Abiquiu and beyond, all the way to southern Colorado. The pink and gray hills, like huge buffalo humps, contrasted with the smoky green of the cottonwoods along the river and made him think of the paintings of Georgia O'Keeffe. Lost in thought, he drove by the Abiquiu Inn on his right and noticed the three crosses high up on the mesa to his left. The crosses, visible from the highway, reached into the sky from their spot behind the penitente morada in the village of Abiquiu.

Then he saw Tessa's gallery up ahead, its front defaced by spirals of red and black paint. The perpetrator had also spray-painted a human skull and written some choice words in black paint: "Jezebel," "Die Bitch Die," "Go Back to Santa Fe," and "Cunt" twice.

"Real friendly neighbors," Fernando said out loud as he pulled into the parking lot in front of the gallery. When he climbed out of his

Cherokee, he spotted Billy sitting off to the side on a rusted five-gallon bucket. Billy's bicycle rested on its kick-stand behind him.

Billy waved.

Fernando waved back and then walked over to where Billy sat on his bucket. "Do you know who did this, Billy?"

Billy shrugged. The youngster wore a Nike T-shirt and shorts, with a Colorado Rockies baseball cap turned backwards on his head. "Some people here don't like her much, I reckon."

"Why's that?" Fernando asked.

Billy shook his head and gave Fernando a hang-dog look. "I don't know. She's real nice to me. I like her okay."

"So do I," Fernando said. Then he walked around the circumference of the building, looking for clues that would lead to the identity of the perpetrator or, more likely, perpetrators.

By the time he'd walked around the gallery, Billy had taken off. He saw the youngster pedaling his bicycle down the highway toward the village.

Before leaving, Fernando sat in his Cherokee for a moment pondering the damage. Anyone who would do something like this must really hate Tessa and could be dangerous. He decided to call Blaine for help. He knew Blaine and Tessa were on the outs, but he needed backup in case he needed to deal with more than Ray Sandoval. At six-five and two hundred and fifty pounds, with a notoriously bad temper, Blaine was an intimidating presence. Not to mention loud and belligerent. Not many people wanted to mess with someone who appeared as bat-shit crazy as Blaine.

Unfortunately, Blaine didn't answer, so Fernando left a message: "Blaine, this is Fernando. Someone spray-painted more threatening slogans on Tessa's gallery here in Abiquiu. I'm on my way to Ojo Caliente, where I think she's staying. I might need your help, so I wanted to give you a heads up. Hang loose, in case I call, okay? I'll talk to you later."

With that, Fernando pulled out on the highway and again took Highway 554 to El Rito and around to Ojo Caliente. The sun had already begun to sink low in the western sky as he crossed the bridge over the Rio Ojo Caliente into the hot springs. Splashes of crimson hugged the hills to the west and plunged the resort into early shadows. He looked for Tessa's CR-V, not knowing the location of Tessa's room. He spotted it at the very end of the Pueblo Suites wing, the farthest from the office. Good for privacy, bad for getting help if you needed it.

Fernando parked beside Tessa's CR-V. He tried to park so that the larger Cherokee would block any view of the CR-V from the entrance in case Ray Sandoval came looking for Tessa here. If little Billy knew Tessa used Ojo Caliente as her place of refuge, then it was likely that others including Sandoval also knew. Sandoval could come calling at any moment. The only question was whether Sandoval would come alone or with a posse.

He looked around to make sure he didn't have company and then knocked on the heavy wooden door of the suite. No response, so he knocked again and waited a couple of minutes. Maybe Tessa hadn't returned to her suite after a late afternoon soak in one of the pools. With that in mind he walked down to the largest pool and then around to the smaller pools. No sign of Tessa in any of them.

Puzzled, Fernando walked back to Tessa's suite. He knocked on the door again, this time hard enough to wake the dead. Suddenly he saw the curtains on the picture window flutter and then move to the side slightly. Tessa was checking out the identity of her visitor.

"Tessa, it's Fernando," he shouted. "Open the door. I've come to help."

Moments later the door opened on Tessa holding a can of pepper spray out in front of her. "What do you want?" she demanded.

"Whoa...I told Ruby I'd come check on you," he said, raising his hand to block the spray if she fired. "Are you okay? I just came from your gallery. Whoever did that could be dangerous. You need to be careful."

"Yeah, no kidding," Tessa shot back. "Tell that to my sister. All she cares about is that I took Jimmy's gun to Blaine's gallery and because of that was somehow responsible for Sonny's murder. How would I know someone would steal the damn gun and shoot Sonny?"

"You wouldn't," Fernando agreed. "She's just angry the two of you are being blamed. Same as you."

Tessa frowned but held the door open for Fernando. "Come in." She let him pass by and then stuck her head out of the door and looked around. Then she locked the door behind her and turned to Fernando.

"Just take a look at this," she said, handing him her cell phone.

Fernando read a text she had highlighted: "Die, bitch, die!"

"They've also called and emailed me the same message," Tessa said. "Real subtle, huh?"

Fernando sat on a chair next to the kiva fireplace. "Who are these guys? Is it just Sandoval?"

"Sandoval and his friends from the village, maybe people who work with him at Ghost Ranch," Tessa said. "I'm not sure how many of them."

"What's their beef?" Fernando asked. "Why are they coming after you?"

Tessa made a face of disgust and sat down on a sofa across from Fernando. "Well, I told you about my philandering, ex-husband Andy who liked to screw married women who felt lonely and neglected. That went over like a lead balloon around here. Then when he got Ray Sandoval's wife pregnant, the threats and hate mail started. To make matters worse, there's the fact that we're outsiders from Santa Fe. The locals hate us almost as much as they hated Georgia O'Keeffe. Imagine that, hating the woman who made Abiquiu famous. Bunch of inbred yokels!"

Fernando winced. "Just a very old community, I guess."

Tessa snorted. "Then why not old enough to know better?"

Fernando shook his head. "I don't know, Tessa. I think people just tend to be bigoted and suspicious of outsiders, sometimes even violent toward them. Human nature, I suppose."

"Yeah, well, Sandoval and his yokels can have it," Tessa said. "I'm taking all my merchandise out of storage in Española and moving it down to either Blaine's or Ruby's gallery in Santa Fe, if they'll get off my back. Or maybe I'll buy my own gallery with Andy's insurance money, I haven't decided."

While they talked, Tessa kept getting up and opening the curtains on the window to check for unwanted visitors. After the third or fourth trip, she asked, "Do you want something to drink? I have red wine and some Coors if you want beer."

"Sure, I'll have a Coors," Fernando said.

Tessa went back to the bedroom bureau and poured herself a glass of red wine and then took a can of Coors out of the mini refrigerator. "I don't have another glass," she said.

"No problem," Fernando said, popping the top. The beer didn't have much taste, but under the circumstances he couldn't complain.

"So what's your plan?" Fernando asked, after the beer started to kick in.

"I need to go back to my gallery tomorrow and get the locked metal box with my deeds and personal records inside," Tessa said. "I didn't take the time this morning—I just wanted to get out of there."

Fernando agreed to accompany her to the gallery tomorrow. At present they decided to go to dinner in the restaurant. After that he could go to the office and get a room for the night. That way they could get an early start tomorrow morning.

Over dinner, they shared Ruby stories. Tessa admitted to being a little afraid of her older sister, who had mothered her when they were teenagers growing up in the Agua Fria neighborhood of Santa Fe. Fernando admitted to having a crush on Ruby all through high school but never having the courage to tell Ruby. "She intimidated every boy at the school," he said, laughing.

"She does that. She still intimidates me," Tessa replied, a little tipsy.

When they finished eating, they went to the front desk only to find that all the rooms were rented for the night. No room at the inn.

"You can sleep on my sofa," Tessa said.

So they returned to Tessa's suite. Fernando brought his Smith & Wesson in from the Cherokee, just in case. In case of what he didn't know and didn't want to think about. Then he called Estelle and told her he wouldn't be home tonight, that he was on a case and spending the night in Ojo Caliente, which was the best face he could put on what he was about to do. What was he about to do?

Estelle reminded him that he was supposed to be retired and hung up on him before he had to elaborate on his bullshit story that stretched the truth to the breaking point. So in the doghouse once again.

Later, when the awkward moment arrived, Tessa brought a spare pillow and blanket over to the sofa. She hesitated for a moment and then said, "You're welcome to sleep with me in the bed. I sleep in the nude, just so you know."

Fernando nodded. "I saw."

He hesitated for a moment and then sat down on the sofa. Finally he stripped down to his T-shirt and shorts and pulled the blanket up to his chin, trying not to think about Tessa.

Tessa went into the bathroom. When she stepped out, she was totally, gloriously nude. Drop-dead gorgeous. She paused for a moment to put lotion on her arms and legs. Then she glanced at Fernando, who was watching her every move. Finally, mercifully, she switched off the light and climbed into the bed by herself.

Unable to get the image of a naked Tessa out of his mind, Fernando began to question his motives once again. Why was he here? What did he want? Was he in self-denial about his attraction to sexy Tessa?

9

Fernando felt soft, warm flesh next to him. He cracked open his eyes expecting to see Estelle sleeping next to him. Instead he saw the shapely bare back and buttocks of a beautiful young woman. What? He struggled awake, trying to remember where he was. Then he remembered: Ojo Caliente, in Tessa Montez's Pueblo Suite. He must have wandered over to her bed from the sofa sometime during the night. Which begged the question: Did they? He felt for his nether parts and was relieved to find he was still wearing his boxers. That was proof, yes? Or was it?

Embarrassed, Fernando climbed out of bed, waking Tessa. He hurried over to the sofa and pulled on his trousers, followed by his shirt and shoes. Fully dressed, he turned to find Tessa smiling at him.

"Don't worry, you were a perfect gentleman," Tessa said, winking.

"Just my luck," Fernando replied. He went into the bathroom and splashed water on his face. Then he stood at the sink wondering what she meant by winking? Did the wink negate Tessa's comment about him being a perfect gentleman? Now he was worried. When he walked out of the bathroom he found Tessa lying on the bed doing stretching exercises, naked as a jaybird.

Feeling agitated, and needing to get away from the temptations of Tessa's all-too-ravishing flesh, he blurted out, "I'm going for coffee."

"Milk and sugar, please," Tessa said as he walked out the door.

Outside, the fresh air invigorated him and cleared his mind. Stay focused. You're here to protect Tessa, not to sleep with her. Or was he kidding himself? Once again he began to doubt his motives.

A few early bathers had gathered in the large pool, soaking in the healing waters. He thought they eyed him suspiciously as he walked by, so he eyed them suspiciously right back.

The restaurant hadn't opened yet, but Fernando found a large commercial coffee dispenser outside in the hallway. He poured himself a cup of coffee, added cream and sugar, and went back outside to the long veranda on the front of the hotel. Taking a seat in one of the wooden chairs, he sipped his coffee and looked over the lush gardens that surrounded the hotel. Finally he began to relax. He realized he had to find a way to extricate himself from this situation before he did something really stupid. Gone was the pretense of helping Tessa. It was time to be honest about his motives. But how to extricate himself? That was the question.

After he finished his first cup, he went back inside and filled two more paper cups with coffee and then grabbed cream and sugars to go. He carried the coffees back to Tessa's suite.

Thankfully, Tessa was completely dressed when she opened the door for him. He could relax, finally. They sat across from each other in the sitting area and made plans for the day. They decided to drive to her gallery right after breakfast so she could look for the metal box containing her personal records. The earlier the better. They wanted to do it quickly before Sandoval or whoever spray-painted and ran-sacked the place could notice their presence.

After finishing their coffee, they walked over to the restaurant and ate breakfast. Fernando, starving, ordered huevos rancheros with extra tortillas. Tessa ordered eggs and toast. By the time they returned to Tessa's suite it was nearly ten o'clock. Time to get moving. They'd just started to get ready for the drive back to Abiquiu when they heard the bellowing:

"TES-SA...TES-SA!"

Tessa rolled her eyes. "Oh God, it's Blaine. What's he want now? I thought I told him to fuck off."

"I have to confess, I called him earlier and told him I was coming up here to help out and that I might need back-up," Fernando said.

Tessa gave him a dirty look.

"He's crazy about you...and sorry for his transgression," Fernando added, although he wasn't sure about either part of that statement. Crazy maybe, but sorry was a stretch for Blaine.

"Yeah, right," Tessa said, opening the curtains to look for Blaine, who was walking down the drive toward Tessa's CR-V. "Here he comes."

Fernando opened the door, noticing Blaine hadn't changed out of his red Bermuda shorts, white T-shirt, and fishing vest. Did he ever change his clothes?

"Where's Tessa? Is she okay?" Blaine asked. The big man's hair was disheveled, a wild look on his face.

"She's fine," Fernando said, holding the door open for Blaine.

Tessa came over to the two of them and addressed Blaine. "Just for the record, I didn't ask for your help, okay?"

"Tess, please! Please forgive me!" Blaine pleaded, his arms open wide as if asking for a big hug. "Goddamnit, I made a mistake, but the skank meant nothing to me. I promise it won't happen again if you take me back. Just one more chance, that's all I'm asking for...."

Blaine's speech of contrition went on for a minute or two while Tessa stood glaring at him, arms crossed. Suddenly she burst out laughing. "Jesus Blaine, are you trying for an Academy Award or what? Enough is enough."

"Ya gotta take me back, Tess," Blaine replied. "My life's shit without you. That goddamn gallery gets lonely by myself. It's you, baby. You're the one for me. I know that now."

"Okay, okay, maybe I will," Tessa said, "but only if you keep it in your pants. No more hooking up with skanks at La Fonda or anywhere else. I already had one philanderer as a husband and I don't want another. I keep saying that, but you don't seem to hear me."

Fernando watched the scene unfold, feeling relieved. Now he could leave knowing Tessa would be protected. He'd go with Tessa this morning to search for her metal box and then quietly bow out. Blaine could handle Sandoval. That wouldn't be much of a match. Blaine topped Sandoval by at least five inches and more than one hundred pounds.

Blaine helped Tessa pack, while Fernando stood back and watched, feeling a bit left out. When finished, Blaine carried the suitcase out to Tessa's CR-V. He was eager to help in order to prove his loyalty to Tessa. By the time they were ready to leave for Abiquiu he and Tessa were tight once again in their on-again, off-again relationship. He offered to drive, but Fernando wanted to take the Cherokee so he could have some measure of control.

"Whatever you say. I bought a new Beretta Ninety after you called yesterday," Blaine said to Fernando. "I left it in my car up by the old hotel. You want me to run up and get it now?"

Fernando shook his head. "I don't think we'll need that. I have my Smith and Wesson in the Cherokee just in case. The fewer the guns, the better."

With that, the three of them climbed into the Cherokee and departed. Fernando drove faster than he normally did. He wanted to get this over with as quickly as possible so he could return to Santa Fe and try to make amends with Estelle. He made it to Abiquiu in half the time it had taken him to drive from Abiquiu to Ojo Caliente yesterday.

"Holy shit!" Blaine said when they sighted the sheer amount of graffiti on Tessa's gallery straight ahead.

"Not pretty, is it?" Fernando replied.

Tessa said nothing. She sat frozen in the front passenger's seat as Fernando pulled into the parking lot. She continued staring at the crude insults without saying a word. She seemed more depressed than angry.

Fernando looked over at her. "Are you okay?"

Tessa sighed. "No...but let's get this over with," she said, opening her door and climbing out. Fernando and Blaine followed.

"So where is this metal box?" Fernando asked.

"In the office locked in a bureau. I just need to find the key—I think it's in my desk," Tessa said, leading the way.

Fernando and Blaine followed Tessa into the gallery. While she and Blaine went into the office to search for the key, Fernando lingered at the door watching for visitors, just in case.

Before long Fernando spotted a gray Ford pickup slowing down and then coming to a stop on the side of the highway. Moments later Ray Sandoval and another man climbed out of the pickup and stood staring at the Cherokee from the road. The other man was short and obese, wearing overalls and a denim baseball cap. Sandoval folded his arms across his chest and said something that made the fat man laugh. Then they continued to stare at Fernando.

"Hurry up, we have visitors," Fernando yelled to Tessa and Blaine, still rummaging in the office.

"Fuck 'em, you want me to get rid of them?" Blaine asked, coming out of the office like a bull.

"Careful, they may be armed," Fernando said.

"Just keep your eyes on them," Tessa said. "Here's the key. I'll have the box in a minute."

Eventually Sandoval and his accomplice got back in their pickup and drove off down the highway east toward the village of Abiquiu. Fernando watched the Ford pickup disappear around a long curve. He worried they hadn't seen the last of Sandoval and his accomplice today.

"Got it," Tessa said. She walked out of the office carrying a metal box that looked about twelve inches square and maybe six inches high. "Are they gone?"

"Looks like it—for the moment anyway," Fernando said, expecting the worst, as usual.

Tessa nodded. "Okay, the other thing I have to do is call a real estate agent this afternoon. My goal is to have the gallery on the market by next week. What do you think?"

"Whoa...slow down. You'll need to replace the windows and clean up the graffiti first," Fernando said. "I know an emergency windows guy in Española. He would come out and measure the windows and then replace them. It wouldn't take him more than a few days."

"And you'll need a good paint stripper for the graffiti," Blaine countered, not to be outdone. "I've used Max Strip before. It's a spray-on and works pretty well, but it'll probably leave the stucco smudged."

"Well, even smudged will look better than it looks now," Tessa said. "I'm thinking Bodes down the street probably has something. You guys wait here, I'll walk down and buy whatever they have and some sponges. Maybe the three of us working together can knock it out this afternoon."

"I'll put the metal box in the back of the Cherokee," Fernando said, taking the box from Tessa. He decided to be a good citizen, in spite of doubting the three of them could clean off the graffiti in one afternoon.

"I'll be back shortly," Tessa said and stepped outside.

Fernando put the box in the rear of the Cherokee and then walked around the gallery to check again on the extent of the graffiti. In back he thought he saw someone on the hill behind the building. He walked half-way up the hill before deciding his eyes had deceived him. Either that or what he saw was a ghost. He neither believed nor disbelieved in ghosts. All he knew was that he'd seen something at Chaco Canyon and Painted Skull Ranch, call it what you will. He had no idea who or what he'd seen on the hill, nor did he care to find out.

When he climbed back down to the Cherokee, he noticed Tessa hadn't yet returned. He turned to Blaine. "Where's Tessa?" he asked, realizing she'd been gone more than enough time to walk to Bodes and back.

Blaine glanced at his watch and then at Fernando with a worried look on his face. "Let's go!"

Fearing the worst, they jumped in the Cherokee. Fernando fired the engine and drove quickly down to Bodes and swerved into the parking lot, both of them in full-blown panic mode now.

Blaine walked around behind Bodes while Fernando ran inside and up to the counter. "Where's the woman who was just in here? Dark hair, bought a can of paint remover."

The clerk winced, an old timer with gray hair and a white handlebar mustache who'd seen his share of trouble over the years and didn't need or want any more. "She just left. Bought a can of Sunnyside graffiti remover and paid for it in cash," he said. "Why're you after her? Is there a problem?"

"Did you see her leave with anyone?" Fernando asked. "Two men in a gray Ford pickup?"

The old timer shook his head. "I never seen anyone with her. She come in by herself and left by herself."

Fernando ran back outside and found Blaine searching behind the building. "I don't see her anywhere," Blaine said.

Not knowing what to do, they climbed back in the Cherokee.

"Which way?" Fernando asked.

Blaine pointed east. "Let's try the village."

Fernando didn't argue. He shot out onto Highway 84 and drove quickly down to the bridge across the Chama River. Just past the bridge he turned right and hit the brake. The Cherokee bounced up the rough road to the top of the mesa, where the adobe walls of the Georgia O'Keeffe House greeted them. Fernando cruised into the village, past Saint Thomas the Apostle Catholic Church and then around to the Penitente Morada on the northeastern corner of the mesa. They saw no trace of the gray Ford pickup anywhere in the village.

"They must have gone west toward Ghost Ranch," Fernando said.

"Hurry up—we'll lose them," Blaine complained.

"I can't go any faster," Fernando said, slowing as they plunged down the road to the mesa. At the bottom of the hill he skidded onto the pavement and shot down Highway 84 past Bodes. Soon Abiquiu Lake came into view off to their left, framed by the massive mesa known as Cerro Pedernal lurking behind it, a dark blue specter. He turned into the entrance to the lake and proceeded down to the large parking lot and picnic grounds, already crowded with people fishing in the lake and picnicking among the tables and fire pits. They drove through the length of the parking lot but didn't find the gray Ford pickup.

Fernando spun around in the parking lot and sped back to the highway. He headed due west toward Ghost Ranch, minutes later turning right onto the primitive road leading into the sprawling property surrounded by distant mesas and jagged cliffs. The road curved around toward the massive Kitchen Mesa, with a maze of roads connecting the various buildings and facilities off to the left, including the stables where Ray Sandoval worked.

Fernando stayed left, following the main loop to the corrals and stables on the northwest side of Ghost Ranch. They circled the loop, passing the campgrounds and the infamous Ghost Cottage where the Archuleta brothers once lived and eventually died. Finally they came to the tumbledown Welcome Center at the end of the loop without seeing the gray Ford pickup anywhere. Fernando pulled over in the parking lot and turned to Blaine.

"I say we continue on up the highway, I don't care if we have to go all the way to Chama," Blaine said. "We have to find Tessa."

"Okay, whatever you say," Fernando said, and followed the primitive road back to Highway 84, where he turned right and headed down the long slope to Monastery Road and the Chama River. Past Monastery Road they entered the long curve that took them around to Echo Amphitheater, a natural echo chamber created by tall red and yellow sandstone cliffs that formed a semi-circle around a flat rocky bottom where tourists liked to stop by to try the echo chamber. A picnic area and hiking trail extended north from the parking lot.

"Look, he's over there!" Blaine said, pointing to the picnic area. Sandoval's gray Ford pickup was parked next to a picnic table at the base of a red cliff near end of the hiking trail.

Fernando hit the brake, causing the Cherokee to skid to the right. Then he swerved to the left into the amphitheater parking lot and coasted to a stop beside the restroom facilities.

Fernando killed the ignition and jumped out of the Cherokee. He followed Blaine, already running down the hiking trail lickety-split. The big man with the pot belly could move surprisingly fast when he wanted to. He looked like a lumbering NFL linebacker going after a quarterback on the opposite team.

Suddenly they heard someone screaming further down the trail: "Fuuuuuuuuuck!" Then a pudgy young man came stumbling down the trail with a handkerchief pressed against his face, covering his eyes. Fernando recognized the screamer as Ray Sandoval's accomplice, the heavy-set man in overalls Fernando had seen with Sandoval back at Tessa's gallery.

"I can't see! Fuck!" the man continued to shout.

Blaine reached the man first. "What's wrong with you?"

"My eyes. I can't see. The bitch sprayed something in my eyes!" the man wailed.

"Tessa?" Blaine asked, grabbing the man by the neck and shaking him roughly. "What did you do to Tessa?"

The man raised his hands high over his head, revealing his red, swollen eyes. "Nothing. I had nothing to do with this. I work for Ray at Ghost Ranch. We were on our way back from Española to buy feed when he saw you in Abiquiu. I have no idea what's going on here. I need water for my eyes. Please!"

Blaine, who stood a foot taller than the man, stared down at him for a moment and then shoved him hard, pitching him in a ditch alongside the trail. "If I find out differently, I'll be back for you," Blaine snarled.

By this time Fernando had caught up with Blaine, who now pointed down the trail.

Then Fernando saw Tessa approaching. She came walking down the paved trail toward them carrying a spray bottle in one hand. With her other hand she gave them the finger.

"Baby, are you okay?" Blaine yelled, running up the trailhead to meet her.

"What took you so long?" Tessa replied, waving the spray bottle at Blaine as if she were about to spray him too.

Fernando kept his distance, not knowing what to expect. Tessa looked angry. Blaine looked confused.

"Where's Sandoval?" Blaine asked.

Tessa pointed behind her toward the gray pickup. "He's back there by the truck. I sprayed him in the face with the paint remover I bought at Bodes. Then I saw a shovel in the bed of his pickup so I grabbed it and hit him over the head with it as hard as I could and took off running."

"What does he want now? Why doesn't he leave you alone?"

"Money...I told you," Tessa said, sounding impatient, like she was talking to a child who refused to understand.

Shaking her head, Tessa made her way calmly to the restroom facilities with her can of spray paint remover, ignoring all of them.

Fernando followed Blaine down the trail into the picnic area. Up ahead they saw Sandoval sitting on his ass, leaning back against the Ford pickup. A ribbon of red blood trickled down the left side of his head onto his ear. Off to the side a shovel lay face down in the dirt.

Sandoval made no effort to get to his feet when he saw them coming. He looked bedraggled, exhausted. "The bitch sprayed me in the face and hit me over the head with a shovel," he said.

"That's nothing compared to what I'm going to do to you," Blaine said. With his left hand he picked up the thin, scraggly Sandoval by his collar and then punched him square in the face with a straight right hand that sent Sandoval flying back against the pickup. Sandoval bounced off the side of the pickup and sprawled face down in the dirt, where he lay motionless.

Blaine went to pick up Sandoval and hit him again, but Fernando intervened, holding him back.

"Enough. He got the message."

10

Tired of Ray Sandoval and everything else associated with Abiquiu, Fernando wanted to return to Santa Fe as fast as possible. First, though, he had to take Tessa and Blaine back to their vehicles at Ojo Caliente, so the two of them could go back to Abiquiu and clean up the graffiti on her gallery. That took nearly an hour. After he dropped them off at the hot springs, Fernando hightailed it back to Santa Fe as fast as the clogged two-lane highway through Española would allow, which wasn't very damn fast. All of which added to his bad mood.

Fortunately Estelle had already gone to bed by the time he finally made it home. When he walked into their kitchen he found a place setting for him on the kitchen table and a note that his dinner was in the refrigerator and needed to be heated in the microwave. He heated the plate of fried chicken and mashed potatoes and wolfed it down with a Modelo from the refrigerator. Finished, he placed the dishes in the sink and tiptoed down the hall and into the bedroom. He undressed and crawled into the bed next to Estelle at the crack of Midnight.

"Bout time," Estelle said and rolled over away from him.

Welcome home. It wasn't the first time he'd come home late and received the cold shoulder treatment.

Next morning, Fernando slept late. He made sure to stay in bed until Estelle left for work at the outreach program. Then he crawled out from underneath the covers and got dressed. He had nothing pressing to do today, so he took his sweet time. After a light breakfast of toast and coffee, he took his second cup of coffee out to the patio. He did his best thinking out on the patio. Something about the cottonwoods along the acequia that always made him feel grounded or maybe protected, he couldn't explain it. A secure place to think, away from the hustle and bustle of the modern world. Now he was getting into the realm of clichés, he realized. But that was how he felt about his patio, cliché or no cliché.

He kept thinking about Becca, the youngest of the three women who worked for Sonny. He hadn't talked to her yet, but it was possible that she could provide some new information. Follow the gun, Raoul Garcia had said. He knew Tessa moved the gun that killed Sonny from Ruby's gallery to Blaine's gallery and that Blaine moved it from his gallery to Sonny's gallery. Once the gun arrived at Athena Gallery, all three of the young women who worked for Sonny had access to the gun, as did Sonny and anyone else who came into Sonny's office. Including the murderer.

He made a decision. First thing this morning he would visit Athena again and question Becca. If she were available. Last time he visited she'd been conveniently absent. He waited until half past ten o'clock and then left the house. He drove down to the Paseo and around to Canyon Road, where he pulled into his old parking lot next to Ruby's gallery. From there he walked to the Athena Gallery and entered through their lush gardens. As he did he saw Athena drive away in a white Lexus. All the better. He would be able to question Becca without Athena's presence.

Fernando saw Mary Margaret at the counter as soon as he stepped inside. She waved awkwardly, and he returned the favor, just as awkwardly. Then he spotted Becca hanging a series of small watercolors along the rear wall. He hadn't met Becca but recognized her from the descriptions he'd been given. Twenty-something, with curly black hair ringed around olive skin, she stood in marked contrast to the other two blondes. He walked back to where she was working and said, "Becca? I'm Fernando Lopez, private investigator. Former private investigator, I should say. I call myself a fixer now."

Turning to face him, Becca said, "I know who you are."

Taken aback, Fernando said, "Good, then you probably know why I'm here."

Becca nodded. "Sonny's murder."

"And the gun that killed him," Fernando replied.

Becca stared at Fernando. "What about the gun?"

"Were you here by any chance when Blaine Rogers brought the gun to Sonny?" Fernando asked.

Becca paused a long moment, considering how to respond. "Actually, yes. I was here the afternoon Blaine brought the gun to Sonny. I heard them talking in the office. Sonny said he didn't want the gun, but Blaine talked him into keeping it for a while. Blaine wanted Sonny to keep it locked up, but Sonny never bothered. He left it right out in the open on his desk, for anyone to see. Sonny wasn't very careful about the gun or anything else, really. He was reckless like that. Reckless, that's the best way I can describe him."

Fernando nodded. "So what happened when the gun was lying on Sonny's desk? Did you see anyone handle the gun?"

Becca winced, as though she were uncomfortable. "We all did. Well, except for Mary Margaret, she's afraid of guns. Sonny took all the bullets out and put them away. The gun wasn't loaded, so we could fool around with it, point it at other people and pretend to shoot them, that sort of thing. Even Sonny got into the act. Everyone thought it was funny, just playing around."

"Funny?" Fernando asked.

Becca blushed. "Like I said, it wasn't loaded."

"What happened to the bullets?" Fernando asked. "Where did Sonny put them when he unloaded the gun?"

"In the top drawer of his desk," Becca said.

This took Fernando by surprise. He considered. "Are you saying that whoever shot Sonny either brought their own ammunition or knew where to find the bullets Sonny had removed from the gun?"

Becca hesitated a moment and then said, "I suppose. The first I knew the gun had been loaded was on the morning I walked in and found the gun on the floor next to Sonny's body."

"So you found the body," Fernando said.

Becca nodded. "It was horrible to walk in and find something like that, Sonny lying on the floor in a pool of blood. I screamed and then ran back outside and called the police with my cell phone."

Just then a couple of tourists walked through the door and began looking around the gallery.

"I really have to get to work," Becca said. "Sorry."

"Here's my card," Fernando said, handing her the card. "Call me any time if you think of something else that might help identify the murderer."

He watched Becca chat with the tourists for a few moments and then left the gallery, as confused as before. So the gun that killed Sonny was on his desk in plain sight and everyone was playing shoot-em-up and having fun with it, including Sonny, who at least had taken the bullets out of the gun. Which begged the question: who reloaded the gun? Whoever reloaded the gun was most likely the killer. That's all he could come up with, given what Becca, Angelica, and Mary Margaret had told him so far. Not much to go on.

As soon as Fernando stepped out of the gallery he saw trouble. A husky man waited for him in the parking lot, sitting on the front of a silver Mercedes coupe with his feet on the front bumper. Resembled an old movie or magazine ad he'd seem somewhere back in the day. The man wore a blue blazer stretched tight over a bulging chest and belly and had the whitest, palest face he'd ever seen, with a shock of light brown hair falling into his eyes. Looked to be in his fifties or early sixties. Well preserved, if pale and flaccid skin could be considered well preserved.

"Mister Lopez," the man said as Fernando approached. "Tom Doering, Athena's brother, I think she may have mentioned me," he introduced himself, holding out his hand.

Fernando shook the man's hand. That explained Doering's look. Another German from Cincinnati.

Doering squeezed Fernando's hand a bit too hard, a tiresome attempt to intimidate. "Do you have a minute?"

"Sure, what can I do for you?" Fernando asked.

"On behalf of my sister Athena, I'd like to ask you to stay out of this case," Doering said. "Leave it to the Santa Fe Police. Let them do what they do and see what develops."

Surprised by Doering's request, Fernando asked, "Why's that? They're not making any progress. Too many fingerprints on the gun that killed Sonny. I have more freedom to investigate, because I don't have to stick so close to the rules, if you know what I mean."

Doering frowned, not liking what he was hearing.

"You do want Sonny's killer brought to justice, right?" Fernando asked. "He was murdered, after all."

Doering shook his head. "Listen, if you want to know the truth, we don't give a damn about Sonny. He was a no-good, wife-beating layabout! He got exactly what he deserved."

"Yes he was," Fernando said, "but he was also your brother-in-law...and he was murdered."

Doering jumped down from the hood of the Mercedes and took a step toward Fernando. "Here's the thing. Athena wants to sell the gallery as fast as possible. She wants out of this provincial, cowboy town. To do that she needs this investigation closed quickly. She doesn't want you or anyone else snooping around looking for dirt, if you know what I mean. More to the point, she's willing to pay you a handsome fee to make sure that happens. You are a fixer, right?"

Fernando stared at Doering. Fixing a situation like this by doing nothing struck him as odd, to say the least. Crazy might be a better word.

"You worked for her before, so why not do it again?" Doering asked. "How does another twenty-five thousand dollars sound?"

Fernando smiled. "Very generous. I'll think about it."

"Good, I'll tell Athena," Doering said and climbed into the Mercedes. He started to drive off and then stopped, rolling down his window. "You need a lift?"

Fernando shook his head.

"Suit yourself," Doering said and drove off down Canyon Road.

11

Fernando walked up Canyon Road to Ruby's gallery, where he'd parked his Cherokee. He opened the front driver's side door and then paused. Maybe he should stop and check on Ruby. He hadn't heard if she and Tessa had reconciled after their quarrel. As far as he knew, Tessa and Blaine were now a ticket, leaving Ruby on the outs. Unless, of course, Tessa and Blaine had already come unglued. Tessa seemed almost as volatile as Blaine.

He closed the car door and walked over to Ruby's gallery. When he opened the heavy front door, he heard Ruby cursing in back. Same old Ruby.

"Oh, it's you," Ruby said when she spotted him.

"Problem?" Fernando asked.

"No, it's just that I cleared all these shelves to make room for Tessa's merchandise and then the bitch decided to take everything to Blaine's gallery instead," Ruby said. "My sister, the ingrate."

Fernando smiled. "I guess they're a ticket again."

Ruby laughed. "Yeah, and how long's that gonna last? That bastard Blaine already cheated on her once with some skank, so what's she thinking? That he'll change his philandering ways and become monogamous? Gimme a break!"

"I hear you," Fernando said. "Still, you might want to leave the shelves empty for now, just in case she changes her mind. She's already changed it twice. You know what they say, three times is a charm."

"Yeah, you're probably right, so fuck it," Ruby said, walking up to meet Fernando.

They moved into the so-called lunch room, where Ruby had

installed a counter and bar stools, along with a mini-refrigerator and a microwave. Ruby brewed each of them a cup of coffee from her Keurig and brought out a small bottle of whole milk and a bowl of sugar, knowing that Fernando liked lots of milk and sugar in his coffee. On the other hand, Ruby preferred her coffee pitch black and strong.

"So have you talked to Tessa since she's been back?" Fernando asked.

Ruby shook her head. "Just briefly, because I think she's trying to avoid me. I know they rented a U-Haul van to go get her stuff from storage in Española. I guess Blaine made room for her merchandise in his gallery. Picasso and Company? Talk about pretentious!"

Fernando added a teaspoon of sugar and a splash of milk in his coffee and stirred the murky liquid.

"What about you? Any news?" Ruby asked.

Fernando shrugged. "I just came from the Athena Gallery. I ran into Athena's brother Tom as I was leaving. He's a piece of work. I don't know quite what to make of him."

Ruby nodded. "He's obnoxious, always putting on that tough guy act. As much as I like Athena, her brother rubs me the wrong way."

"He offered me twenty-five thousand dollars to stop my investigation into who killed Sonny," Fernando added.

"What? You're kidding. Twenty-five thousand dollars to stop investigating? What are they trying to hide?" Ruby asked.

"That's the question," Fernando replied. "His explanation was that Athena wants the investigation to end quickly so she can sell the gallery as soon as possible."

Ruby frowned but said nothing.

"I also talked to Becca, the youngest of the women who work at Athena Gallery," Fernando said. "She said when Blaine gave the gun to Sonny for safe keeping, Sonny left it out in the open on his desk and that all of them played with the gun, pointed it at each other and pretended to shoot."

"With a loaded gun?" Ruby asked, incredulous.

Fernando shook his head. "No. She said Sonny removed the bullets."

"Wait a minute," Ruby responded. "If the gun wasn't loaded, then how did it shoot and kill Sonny?"

"Apparently the murderer either brought the ammunition with them or found the bullets that Sonny had taken out of the gun," Fernando said. "I was told Sonny kept the bullets in the top drawer of his desk."

"I don't know, Fernando, maybe you should just take the twenty-five grand and forget about it," Ruby said, shaking her head. "It just gets weirder the more I hear about it."

Fernando laughed.

Just then the front door of the gallery opened. "Shit!" a woman's voice rang out, followed by the door slamming closed.

Ruby lowered her head, recognizing the voice.

"Tessa?" Fernando asked.

Sure enough, Ruby's younger sister rounded the corner and burst into the lunch room. Wearing dirty white shorts and an even dirtier white T-shirt, with her face smudged with dirt and her dark hair tied back under a blue bandana, Tessa looked like a pirate who'd been swabbing decks all day. A veritable mess.

"I need help," Tessa said. "I need someone to help me move the last load of my stuff down from Española to Blaine's gallery. Fucking Blaine says he threw his back out this morning and can't make another run. I think he's just drunk, he's been drinking all day long."

"Hah! I told you Blaine was a worthless drunk!" Ruby shot back.

Tessa raised her arms. "Don't start, Ruby...I'm hot, I'm dirty, I'm tired, and I'm in no mood to be lectured. Right now I just need one of you guys to help me move my last load."

"I have a gallery to run here, I can't just walk out," Ruby replied.

Both Tessa and Ruby turned to Fernando.

Fernando shrugged. "Well, I suppose I could help out. How long would this take?"

"No more than an hour, hour and a half max," Tessa said.

"Okay," Fernando said. He finished his coffee and followed Tessa outside. Parked alongside his Cherokee sat a new U-Haul Cargo Van, its orange and blue logo glowing on a shiny white background.

Tessa climbed into the driver's seat and waited for Fernando. Once he'd buckled up, she pulled out on Canyon Road and drove down to the Paseo and around to the entrance to Highway 84/285. On the highway she hit the gas, speeding by the Santa Fe Opera and the Tesuque turn-off. The speedometer hovered somewhere around 90 m.p.h. while she wove in and out of traffic, passing everyone except a young kid driving a red Mustang with a dented fender and a cracked windshield. When Tessa tried to pass the Mustang, the kid hit the gas and zoomed ahead of her. Tessa cursed like a truck driver and gave the kid the finger.

"What's your hurry?" Fernando asked.

Tessa gave him a dirty look but said nothing.

They raced through the Pojoaque commercial strip and entered the junky outskirts of Española, Tessa still giving him the silent treatment. That was okay with Fernando. He had nothing to say to her either. In retrospect, he'd decided Tessa was just as difficult as Ruby. Her tongue was every bit as sharp and her choice in men was just as bad, if not worse.

They turned north on Highway 68, known as the Low Road to Taos, in order to distinguish it from the High Road to Taos, which cut through the Sangre de Cristo Mountains. The Low Road to Taos followed the Rio Grande as it wound its way north through the Rio Grande Valley. Before they caught sight of the river, Tessa turned left on a commercial side street that dead-ended at a self-storage lot. The lot contained dozens of concrete self-storage lockers with heavy steel doors.

Tessa stopped at a locker halfway down the back row and switched off the engine. She jumped out of the panel truck and unlocked the metal door. Fernando joined her, helping pull back the heavy steel door that creaked loudly every inch of the way. Inside the locker he saw a scattering of boxes holding pottery, kachina dolls, and other Southwestern arts and crafts. A stack of Navajo style rugs had been thrown against the back wall, on top of a plastic swimming pool for little kids. Since he didn't see any little kids around, he figured the plastic swimming pool was intended to hold the rugs. Hell of a way to transport rugs, if you asked him. On a more positive note, it looked to Fernando like they could fit everything in the back of the panel truck without any difficulty. Everything but the plastic swimming pool, which would have to stay in the locker for the next renter.

Suddenly Fernando saw movement out of the corner of his eye. Something had moved in front of the locker two doors down. Then he saw an elderly man step out of the locker, stagger, and grab the door to steady himself. The man looked ancient, his face resembling a saguaro cactus: all pits and crevices. Wearing several layers of shirts over dirty denim jeans, the old timer continued to hold on to the side of the locker for support. Fernando worried the old man was about to fall over.

Tessa noticed Fernando staring at the old man. "That's Pops," she said, "he lives in his locker."

"Hi Missus!" Pops shouted to Tessa, who waved back.

Fernando walked over to the old man's locker. "You live here?"

"Yessir," Pops said and tapped the side of the locker under the number 14. "That's my address, fourteen skid row," he said, chuckling.

Inside Fernando saw a dirty mattress on the floor, a cane-back chair held together by duct tape, and a Styrofoam cooler.

Fernando shook his head. "Don't you have any kin? Anyone you could stay with?"

"All dead," the old man said. "Every last one of them, even my kids."

Fernando looked around and then asked, "Where's your restroom?"

"The loo?" Pops pointed down toward the river. "Pick any tree you want. Be careful where you step, though." Here he chuckled again. "They don't smell too good either!"

Fernando rolled his eyes. The country had gone to hell. Hundreds of homeless people lived on the streets in Santa Fe, thousands in Albuquerque, the largest city in the state. Meanwhile other people lived in million-dollar homes, especially in Santa Fe. It was the *Grapes of Wrath* all over again. Something had to give. The disparity between rich and poor was too great. It couldn't go on like this forever. Sooner or later the country had to explode.

"Stay away from number twenty," Pops warned, pointing down the row of lockers. "Guy who lives there ain't right in the head. He's got a long gun in there. I think he might be dangerous."

Fernando walked back to Tessa's locker. "Let's load the stuff and get the hell out of here."

Tessa nodded, opening the side and rear doors of the panel truck. They took turns carrying boxes from the storage locker to the truck.

Though small and slender, Tessa proved much stronger than she looked and every bit as capable as Fernando at carrying the heavy boxes. Between the two of them, it didn't take long at all. Fifteen minutes later the locker was empty except for the rugs in the plastic swimming pool. Fernando grabbed the rugs in one large bundle and tossed them into the truck on top of the boxes. They had everything except the swimming pool.

"Do you want the swimming pool?" Fernando asked.

"No, leave it. It was here when I rented the locker."

Tessa removed the bandana from her wild black hair and wiped the sweat from her forehead. Then she stuffed the bandana in her rear pocket and locked the door of her locker.

Before leaving, Tessa went over to Pops and handed him a ten-dollar bill. "Thanks for your help, Pops."

"I didn't really help none," Pops said.

"Sure you did," Tessa said, smiling. She gave Pops a pat on the back and then climbed into the panel truck. Fernando joined her, waving goodbye to Pops as Tessa drove off. She stopped at the self-storage office and dropped off the key to her locker and then turned onto Highway 68.

"Pops is a kind old man... just fallen on hard times," Tessa said.

"I gathered," Fernando replied.

They didn't say another word on the way back to Santa Fe. Fernando leaned back on his headrest and tried to relax, but he kept thinking about what it must be like to actually live in a self-storage locker. The more he thought about it, the angrier he got that so many people were allowed to live on the street in a country this wealthy. Filthy will wealth.

In Santa Fe Tessa drove straight to Blaine's Picasso and Company gallery on Canyon Road. They parked in the side lot and climbed out of the panel truck. Fernando stretched his legs for a few seconds and then followed Tessa into the gallery that for him was haunted. The gallery brought back so many memories of Jimmy Mackey, Ruby's late ex-husband who showed most of his work at Picasso and Company and who was murdered in Taos. Both good and bad memories of Jimmy flooded over Fernando as he lagged behind Tessa, lost in thought.

Several of Jimmy's famous Chopped Nudes paintings still hung on the walls of the front room. The dull, rudimentary landscapes meant for the tourist crowd paled by comparison to Jimmy's colorful images of arms and legs protruding from various female body parts. Jimmy had a vivid, some might say deranged, imagination. But say what you will about the crazy bastard, Jimmy was the real deal, a true artist who lived to create his strange images.

Tessa led the way into the office, where Blaine had been sitting at his desk with a bottle of tequila and a tall glass. When Blaine saw them coming, he jumped up and bent over. Grabbing his lower back in his best pantomime, he said, "You know I'd help if I could, but I threw my back out this morning. Hurts like hell. Yeah, I might have to go over to Urgent Care."

"Uh-huh," Tessa said.

"Owww!" Blaine said, apparently trying to win an Academy Award. "Even hurts to walk."

"Stop the act, Blaine," Fernando said. "You're just lazy or drunk."

"Try both," Tessa added.

"Well, fuck off, both of you," Blaine responded, sitting back down at the desk and pouring himself a half-glass of tequila.

"I'll help you bring the boxes in," Fernando said to Tessa.

"Put the boxes in the back room for now," Blaine said. "We'll have to find space for them in the gallery."

So Fernando and Tessa carried in the boxes one at a time and placed them in the back room, with no help from Blaine, who continued to drink. When finished, Tessa offered to give Fernando a ride up to his Cherokee outside Ruby's gallery. "The least I can do," she said.

"No thanks, I'll just walk to clear my mind," Fernando said, stepping outside, eager to get away from the bickering couple. The proverbial bloom was off the rose. He would give them two months, not a day more.

Blaine was a lazy drunk and ne'er-do-well, while Tessa was a lit fuse about to explode.

12

Fernando woke up with a barking lower back. Ironically, his back-ache was exactly what Blaine had faked yesterday afternoon. He cursed Tessa and her lazy paramour Blaine for enticing, luring, and beguiling him to transport and carry Tessa's heavy boxes from Española to Blaine's gallery. What was he thinking? Why didn't he insist Blaine get off his fat ass and carry the boxes? If he ever saw Blaine or Tessa again it would be too soon. He washed his hands of both of them. The two of them deserved each other

In considerable pain, Fernando first took a hot shower and let the jets of hot water caress his back. Then he stepped out of the shower and rubbed Ted's Pain Cream over his lower back, a miracle cure Estelle had discovered after injuring her back in a fall one snowy day last winter. Ted's Cream helped, as did an Aleve he popped before leaving the bathroom, trying to avoid looking in the mirror so that he wouldn't age, as was his superstition. About the only time he glanced in the mirror was when he shaved with his electric razor, and then only quickly, eyes half closed. He'd glimpsed his wrinkled face and salt and pepper hair enough times, thank you.

Feeling better, Fernando walked to the kitchen and thankfully found a half pot of coffee Estelle had left for him. He heated a cup of coffee in the microwave and took it out to the patio along with his cell phone to check the latest headlines. He'd just taken a seat on his patio bench when his cell phone rang. He didn't recognize the caller ID but answered it anyway.

"Mr. Lopez, it's Mary Margaret from the Athena Gallery," a disembodied voice responded. The voice sounded far way, dispirited.

"Yes, I remember," Fernando said. "What can I do for you?"

After a long pause, Mary Margaret said, "I wondered if we could talk somewhere outside the gallery. I have some information about Becca. I thought you might want to know."

"Becca? Okay, when and where do you want to meet?" Fernando asked.

"I can meet you today on my lunch hour," Mary Margaret said. "Would Noon on the Plaza work for you?"

"Sure," Fernando said, hearing her click off as he spoke, as if she were calling surreptitiously. Which might explain the muted voice.

He finished his coffee while brooding about Mary Margaret and why she was so circumspect, if that was the right word for her less than forthcoming attitude. Then he went inside and grabbed a stale croissant from Estelle's breadbox, which he devoured with another cup of coffee. By then he'd ingested enough caffeine to at least begin the day.

Fernando locked the house and then went for a leisurely walk along Acequia Madre, which helped loosen his back. By the time he returned his watch registered a quarter past eleven, so he made himself a cheese and green chile sandwich and washed it down with another cup of coffee. After he cleaned up the kitchen, he set the alarm system and left the house. He drove the Cherokee down to the Paseo and around to Alameda Street, where he always parked when downtown.

Today the damned tourists had taken all his usual parking places on Alameda. He ended up way down past Shelby Street. Grumbling to himself, he walked up Shelby to the Plaza. He saw Mary Margaret sitting by herself on a bench near the bandstand. She appeared to be eating a container of yogurt. When she finished, she put the empty container and a spoon in a paper bag and closed it tight. She smiled when she spotted Fernando walking down the sidewalk past the bandstand.

"Mary Margaret," he said, approaching the bench. He noticed the telltale wrinkles around her eyes and mouth. Early forties, he guessed. That would seem to be too old for Sonny's taste in women, given what he knew about Sonny.

"Mister Lopez, thanks for coming," Mary Margaret replied, scooting over on the bench to make room for him. Then she looked him over carefully. "Not to be critical, but you don't look like a professional private investigator. I mean the usual type you see in the movies."

Fernando glanced down at his jeans and Eddie Bauer sun shirt. "I'm retired," he said, not pleased by her comment. He'd never claimed to be a Hollywood version of a private investigator or anything else. "So what's up? You said you wanted to talk about Becca?"

Mary Margaret nodded. "I heard what she told you the other day, and I wanted to correct some of what she said. She's right about Blaine bringing the gun to our gallery, but the first time Angelica and I actually saw the gun Becca was playing with it on Sonny's desk. No one else played with it, just her. Sonny got angry when he saw Becca fooling around with the gun because it was still loaded. He took the gun away from her and removed the bullets."

"What happened to the bullets?" Fernando asked.

"Sonny put the bullets somewhere in his desk," Mary Margaret said. "We never saw them again."

Saying nothing, Fernando let her talk.

"Not only that, but this idea that all of us enjoyed playing with the gun and pretending to shoot each other just isn't true," she continued. "After Sonny removed the bullets, he only allowed Becca to play with the gun. She was Sonny's favorite, the youngest of the three of us. She was the one he usually asked to stay after hours. And she loved the attention, she loved every minute of it. Sonny treated her like a queen. He let her take extra days off, long lunch breaks, whatever she wanted. No other employer would ever put up with all the days of work she missed. She even misses days now, after Athena took over the gallery. I don't know what that's all about. Angelica and I don't understand why Becca gets special treatment."

Now Fernando was interested. "Tell me about Athena. What's it like working for her?"

Mary Margaret shook her head. "I don't know her that well. She's a lot more efficient than Sonny, but like Sonny she's more interested in money than running the gallery. Ever since Sonny's death she's wanted to sell the gallery quickly and take the money."

"Did she know Sonny was also trying to unload the gallery— before he was murdered?"

"Yes, they fought about it nonstop," Mary Margaret said.

"Sometimes Sonny would yell so loud at her over the phone that we had to close the office door so customers wouldn't hear him yelling. It was embarrassing."

Fernando smiled. "Quite a pair."

She ignored his comment.

"So they were fighting like cats and dogs before Sonny's murder," Fernando said, mostly to himself, trying to get the timeline straight in his mind.

Mary Margaret nodded. "Yes, as soon as she found out Sonny wanted to sell the gallery. She was worried he wouldn't get a fair price."

Fernando nodded. "Here's another question. How and when did Athena find out Sonny had been murdered?"

"Yeah. I called her the morning Becca and Angelica found him. As soon as the police were done asking us questions, I called Athena."

"Hmmm, Becca told me she found Sonny, she didn't mention Angelica," Fernando said.

"Well, they arrived at the same time, but I think Becca did enter the gallery first," Mary Margaret said. "When I arrived, Becca was weeping nonstop. She made a terrible scene. So I had to call Athena and tell her the news."

"What was Athena's reaction when you told her Sonny was dead?" Fernando asked.

"Subdued," Mary Margaret said. "I was surprised she was so composed. She just thanked me for calling and hung. Very strange."

Fernando began to ask another question when Mary Margaret pointed to the corner of the Plaza, where Tom Doering was crossing San Francisco Street from the La Fonda Hotel.

"I told them where I was going," Mary Margaret said, blushing. "I guess I shouldn't have. I don't much like Tom."

Tom marched over to the bench, a sour look on his pale, pudgy face. "They need you back at the gallery right away," Tom said to Mary Margaret. "Someone wants to buy Tommy Macaroni's painting of the yellow sunflower. No one can find the adjusted sales price."

Mary Margaret nodded, gathering together her purse and lunch bag. She walked off quickly without a word, head lowered.

Staring at Tom's face Fernando asked, "Don't you people in Cincinnati ever get any sun?"

Tom frowned. "So it looks like you aren't interested in our offer," he said, ignoring Fernando's question.

"I haven't decided," Fernando replied. "Maybe yes, maybe no."

"Time to make up your mind," Tom said.

"Tell me...has Athena received any offers to buy the gallery?" Fernando asked. "I hear she's been trying to sell it as fast as possible. Ever since she found out that Sonny was trying to sell it, right?"

"So what?" Tom shot back.

"A divorced couple fighting over an expensive piece of property can get nasty," Fernando said. "Just how nasty is the question."

Tom balled his fists and took a step forward. "Listen, I got no patience for nickel and dime characters like you. If you know what's good for you, you'll take the twenty-five thousand and get lost."

Fernando took a deep breath. He tried his best to control his temper, which wasn't easy in the present circumstances. He didn't take kindly to being insulted by arrogant buffoons like Tom Doering. "Is that how you do it in Cincinnati? Just throw your money around and hope you can buy people off?"

"Look, my sister just wants to sell the gallery and get out of this fucking border town," Tom said angrily.

"Border town?" Fernando exploded. He sprang up and poked the pudgy man hard in the chest. "Watch your mouth, you ignorant prick! Santa Fe was founded in sixteen ten—it's the oldest state capitol in the country. The sooner people like you stop coming here, the better off we'll be."

Taken aback, Tom backed up and then looked around as if worried about creating a scene in a 'border' town. He was all show and no fight. A lightweight pretending to be a heavy.

"Too many brown people for you?" Fernando asked, goading Doering. He wanted Doering to throw the first punch. Just one. That's all he would need in order to finish this business once and for all.

Tom started to say something and then stopped. Instead, he turned and walked away, looking back to make sure Fernando wasn't following him.

Fernando watched the pudgy man walk across San Francisco Street and disappear into the La Fonda Hotel. Good riddance.

13

His encounter with Tom Doering put Fernando in a bad mood. He was going to the dark place, where guilt and remorse from a lifetime of violent confrontations and bad juju lurked just beneath the surface of his consciousness, threatening to erupt at any moment. After one nightmarish murder of a ten-year-old child by an abusive stepfather a few years back, Estelle had sent him to a psychiatrist who'd prescribed an anti-depressant. He took the medication for two weeks before realizing it made him feel like a zombie. Like the walking dead. So he flushed the medication down the toilet without telling Estelle. Since then he'd been able to control his dark moods, more or less, by going for long walks and frequenting Happy Hour at El Farol with his Canyon Road friends.

So suck it up, he told himself. He sat on the bench for a few minutes watching the Plaza fill up with tourists. Finally he decided that since he was downtown, he might as well check with Manny at the Washington Avenue Station to see if he'd turned up anything new in his investigation of Sonny's murder. He crossed the street to Washington Avenue and walked the two blocks to the station. He was surprised when he walked in and found his old friend Linda at the front counter. Linda had retired months ago. Was he having a flashback or what?

"What are you doing here?" Fernando asked, noticing that Linda had stopped coloring her hair. Her long dark hair, now streaked with gray and wound in a tight braid, fell half-way down her back. And she was wearing dark glasses, which he hadn't seen before.

"Well I'm glad to see you too," Linda fired back.

An old hippie who'd moved to Santa Fe after getting tired of living at the New Buffalo Commune in Taos where there were more gurus than followers, Linda had a killer sense of humor. They'd had a brief affair some twenty years ago but broke it off to save their friendship—and his marriage. It was Fernando's only indiscretion in forty years of marriage. Until Tessa. If, indeed, Tsssa had been an indiscretion and not just a temptation.

"Yeah, Brad bailed," Linda continued. He took off with his girlfriend to Pagosa Springs in order to get ready for the ski season. I'm back until they can find a permanent replacement."

"Great...or rather, my sympathy," Fernando replied.

Linda laughed. "I need all the sympathy I can get. This place is crazier then ever. Now Manny is talking about retiring. Even the Chief is getting burned out."

"Is Manny in his office?"

Just then Linda's phone rang. "Yes, your old office," she said, pointing down the hallway.

Fernando walked back to the familiar office, which looked much the same as it did in his day. Same poor lighting, same ugly metal furniture, same dirty window that wouldn't open, and same mess of paperwork covering every surface in the office. The only difference he saw was that the discarded food wrappers now were Lotaburger instead of Great American Burrito Company. A step up? Or maybe down, depending on how you looked at it.

"You could have at least cleaned up my mess before you moved in yours," Fernando said, walking into the office.

"Hah!" Manny said, sitting back in a chair with his feet on the desk. "I gave up. I found paperwork from Padilla, the guy before you. This office is like a fucking museum. Or a mausoleum."

Fernando laughed. "Law enforcement and organization, not a good fit."

"Law and dis-order, that's what it should be called, for sure," Manny joked.

"Speaking of dis-order, what's new on the Sonny Davis murder?" Fernando asked.

"Nothing," Manny replied. "Absolutely nothing. Everyone's guilty, or no one's guilty, who knows?"

"What do you mean?" Fernando asked.

"Well, everyone's fingerprints are on the gun, including the victim's—Sony, Ruby, Tessa, Blaine, Mary Margaret, Angelica, and Becca. Pretty much every one of them hated and had a motive to murder the despicable bastard. To make matters worse, the gallery has a security system, but no video. So we have no hard evidence that points to any one of them. The Chief won't touch the case. It's bad publicity for the city when one of its major galleries is involved in a murder investigation. The last time he had a case like this, the mayor called him into his office and gave him hell."

"What about Sonny's fuck buddy, as you called her?" Fernando asked. "The woman—I'm assuming it was a woman—who Sonny had sex with on the night he was murdered?"

"Forensics found nothing on the Taos sofa or in the gallery that would identity her," Manny responded. "Her DNA doesn't match any of the three young women who work at the gallery."

Fernando frowned. "Have you checked out Athena Doering? She and her brother are in town now. I hear that Athena and Sonny were fighting over selling the gallery before he was murdered."

Nodding, Manny said, "Yeah, but they arrived the day after Sonny was murdered. We checked their airline tickets."

"So what's next?" Fernando asked.

Manny shrugged. "I suppose it'll become another cold case. One of many. Seems like the pile is growing faster than ever these days. I don't know why."

Fernando bit his tongue. He had a few opinions on why, but didn't want to share them with Manny. It wasn't Manny's fault the Chief was afraid of touchy cases involving rich gallery owners and the over-class in general. Scared stiff that some fat cat would come after his job if he rubbed them the wrong way.

"What do you hear from Antonio?" Manny asked, changing the subject to something more pleasant.

"Not much," Fernando said. "I guess he likes being alone out there in his cabin in the Pecos. I couldn't stand it. I'd go crazy."

"Me too. Like I said before, I hate fishing and camping," Manny said. "Not my cup of tea."

They swapped Antonio stories for a few minutes before Manny had to leave for a meeting with the Chief. "Wish me luck," Manny said.

"Yeah...and let me know if anything does break in the Sonny Davis case, okay?" Fernando asked.

"Will do."

Fernando walked down the long hall to the front door. Linda was again on the phone, frantically taking notes from a caller. She managed to wave as he walked by. He waved back.

Outside, Fernando was happy to be out of the station. He had no nostalgia for his days as lead detective. Too many bad memories: friction with the Chief and an endless stream of people with problems. Not surprising that flashbacks sometimes took him back to the dark place.

Crossing the Plaza Fernando happened to see a Sotheby's For Sale sign in the window of one of the galleries. The sign brought him back to the status of Athena Gallery. He began to wonder if Sonny had in fact put Athena Gallery on the market before his death, as Fernando kept hearing. When he came to the end of Shelby Street he crossed Alameda Street and took a seat on one of the stone benches along the Santa Fe River.

He decided the quickest way to find out about the status of the gallery would be to call a real estate agent. So he took out his cell phone and called Diane Ortiz, a good friend of Estelle's who worked as a real estate agent for RE/MAX. It took him a while to find her cell phone number on his Recents list. The last time he'd called her was about a dinner party months ago. He clicked on her number.

"This is Diane Ortiz," she answered right away.

"Hi Diane, this is Fernando Lopez calling," he responded.

"Fernando! Is everything all right with you and Estelle?" Diane asked. "Every time I get a call from an old friend, they're either in the hospital or someone in the family has just passed."

Fernando laughed. "No, nothing like that. Estelle and I are fine. I'm just calling to ask if you can find out if Athena Gallery has gone on the market."

"Sure. That's the one on Canyon Road, right? Owned by the former soccer player who was just murdered?"

"Right," Fernando said.

"Okay, let me look at my listings," Diane said, pausing for several seconds. "Yes, here it is. Must be a fire sale. It's listed at two point nine million, which seems low for a building that size on Canyon Road."

"Can you tell me when Sonny put it on the market?"

"Sure, let me look at the MSL listing," she said.

Fernando waited impatiently.

"Two weeks ago, looks like," Diane said. "Except Sonny didn't put it on the market."

"Then who did?" Fernando asked.

"Athena Doering."

"Are you sure?" Fernando asked.

"Yes, Sonny's not even listed here," Diane said.

14

Fernando arrived late for Happy Hour at El Farol. When he'd returned from downtown he discovered a shopping list that Estelle had left for him this morning, so he had to go back downtown to the Shed for a jar of red chile and to the their grocer for blue corn tortillas and other ingredients Estelle needed for her famous blue corn beef enchiladas with red chile. By the time he drove up Canyon Road and parked in the lot across the street from El Farol his watch read half past four.

He crossed Canyon Road and approached an ancient homeless guy panhandling on the steps of El Farol, Wearing tattered jeans and a dirty gray sweatshirt, the old geezer wore a dusty U.S. Army, Vietnam Veteran baseball cap pulled down low over his forehead. He raised his hand when Fernando approached and said, "I won't bullshit you, I need beer money."

Fernando stopped on the bottom step.

"How's about I sit down at one of the tables here on the porch and you bring me out a cold one? They won't allow me inside."

Fernando sighed and handed the man a ten dollar bill. "Take it to the grocery store down the hill. Get yourself a beer and something to eat."

The old timer smiled, revealing missing front teeth. "Much obliged, mister. You have yourself a good day."

Fernando watched the old man amble down Canyon Road clutching the ten dollar bill in his right hand. A good day? Been a while since he'd had one of those. In fact, Fernando couldn't remember the last time he'd had a day to brag about. Or was he just misremembering and being a goddamn grouch, as Estelle told him whenever he complained about his day? Lighten up, get happy, he told himself, and walked into El Farol for Happy Hour.

He heard Ruby's loud voice as soon as he stepped inside the door of El Farol. "What the fuck, Blaine? Do you have to do that here, right in front of everyone? Are you some kind of exhibitionist?"

Penny, one of the day bartenders, shook her head and pointed to the restaurant part of El Farol. Fernando saluted and walked through archway.

"Look at that—can you believe them?" Ruby asked Fernando when he entered the dining room. She pointed to Blaine and Tessa, who sat across from Ruby at their usual table by the colorful Flamenco Dancers mural on the wall. Tessa straddled Blaine with her arms wrapped around his neck. The two noodled each other, oblivious to everyone around them and apparently unaware of how ridiculous they looked to everyone else in El Farol.

Penny followed Fernando and placed his usual Modelo draft on the table in front of him.

Ruby sat at the far end of the table, as far away as possible from the amorous couple, with Dave Stein and Athena Doering.

Blaine freed himself from Tessa for a moment and came up for air. "You're just jealous because you can't hold a man," he said to Ruby. "Never could. Not even Jimmy Mackey."

Ruby's face turned red. "Hah! I haven't found a man I'd want to hold, least of all you! And by the way, I left Jimmy before he left me!"

Tessa cursed. "Can't you just wish us well, big sister? Isn't that what big sisters are supposed to do?"

Ruby turned to Fernando. "You see what I mean?"

Fernando shrugged, not wanting to get involved in yet another of Ruby's arguments.

Dave Stein cleared his throat. An eighty-something artist, Dave wore the same blue suit he'd worn for at least twenty years again today. He had tufts of gray hair growing out of his ears and on the top of his otherwise bald head. When he talked, he spoke out of the corner of his mouth, like a ventriloquist without a dummy. He was both ventriloquist and dummy.

"Wha'd they say?" Dave croaked. "What in the hell are they doing over there anyway?"

"Yeah, why don't you get a hotel room?" Ruby added.

"What hotel? Where are they goin'?" Dave asked.

Ruby threw up her arms. She turned to Dave and started to say something but then changed her mind. Instead, she shook her head in defeat.

Trying to ignore the bickering, Fernando turned to Athena. "So I see you put your gallery up for sale two weeks before Sonny was murdered."

Athena, taken by surprise, hesitated a moment. "Yes...I found out he was about to sell for a fraction of what it's worth...just to get rid of it, so he could go back to England. I felt I had no choice."

"But how could you sell the gallery?" Fernando asked. "You were the minor partner, owning only forty-five percent."

"Yes, but my lawyer inserted a clause in the contract that I'm sure Sonny never took the time to read," Athena said. "It gives me control of the gallery in case of malfeasance or dereliction that would endanger the physical premises or monetary value of the property. I had my lawyer add that to be on the safe side because Sonny could be so careless and irresponsible. We filed for malfeasance as soon as I heard Sonny was about to sell the gallery cheap."

Fernando nodded, at the same time both suspicious and impressed by her take-charge attitude. She wanted what she wanted and was not about to lose money on her gallery.

"So you spoke with Tom about our predicament," Athena said. "We can't have this investigation hanging over our heads, because we need to sell the gallery quickly. Have you made a decision about what you're going to do? Will you help us?" Athena asked.

Fernando shook his head. "You want to pay me twenty-five thousand dollars to stop investigating, is that right?"

Athena shrugged. "You are a fixer, yes? Well, that's how you can fix this. You can leave it alone. Just walk away."

"Let sleeping dogs lie, eh?"

She gave him a dirty look.

"You don't care or want to know who killed Sonny, I get that. But why?" Fernando asked. "There must be a reason. I'm trying to figure out just what that reason might be."

Athena sighed and looked off in the distance for a moment and then turned back to Fernando. "I wonder," she said. "What does it matter? He's dead...and most of us who knew him are glad he's dead. That might sound like a terrible thing to say, but it's the truth. So what difference does it really make who killed him? What will knowing the identity of the person who killed him accomplish? It won't bring him back from the dead, will it?"

"What about justice?" Fernando asked.

"For whom? For Sonny, or for the people he abused all his life? What about his victims?" Athena shot back, suddenly getting angry. "Why are you so concerned with someone that despicable?"

Fernando frowned. He had no answer to that.

After taking a few moments to calm herself, Athena continued by saying, "I should tell you that Tom doesn't take no for an answer. Just so you know before you make a decision."

Fernando laughed. "Is that a warning or a threat?"

Athena shrugged. "Take it as you will."

So he took it as a threat, because that's what it sounded like.

Fernando did not like to be threatened. It brought out the worst in him. So he decided then and there that he would not only not walk away from the investigation but that he would do whatever it took to find out who killed Sonny. Whatever it took. However long it took.

Fernando finished the remainder of his Modelo in silence. Then he stood up and looked down at Athena. "You can tell Tom the answer is no, and if he has a problem with that, he knows where to find me."

With that Fernando walked out of El Farol without looking back.

15

So then the war of intimidation began. Fernando saw the silver Mercedes everywhere, like the Grim Reaper lurking in the shadows ready to pounce. It took him a day or so before he realized it was Tom Doering's Mercedes. Sometimes Doering was alone, and sometimes he was with a companion riding shotgun. He saw the Mercedes driving by his house on Acequia Madre and driving by Ruby's studio on Canyon Road. Even parked in the El Farol parking lot across from the restaurant. The in-your-face, cat and mouse game lasted all week.

Then sitting on his patio with a cup of coffee one morning Fernando received a phone call from his tormentor. He clicked the decline button on his cell phone, but Doering kept calling every few minutes. Tired of the noise, he muted the sound on his phone, but still the damn cell phone buzzed and danced around on the goddamn wooden bench until finally Fernando hit the accept button.

"What do you want, Doering?" Fernando barked into the phone.

"How about we talk," Doering said, ignoring Fernando's obvious displeasure. "Try to work something out between the two of us before this escalates. What do you say?"

"What do we have to talk about?" Fernando shot back.

"Come on, Lopez, you know what we need to talk about," Doering said. "How about we meet for lunch at La Plazuela in La Fonda, say Noon. Lunch is on me. What do you have to lose?"

Against his better judgment, and hoping to get rid of Doering once and for all, Fernando said, "I'll be there."

As soon as he clicked off he began having second thoughts. Lunch with an unsavory character like Doering was the last thing he wanted to do today. On the other hand maybe it was better to get it all out—listen to the man and try to end the jousting match. It wasn't as though he were about to break the case wide open, so what were they worried about? If Manny and his Forensics team couldn't do it, how could he? It didn't figure.

He busied himself working around the house until late morning. Before leaving he strapped on his Smith & Wesson in its open carry holster, just to be prepared for whatever eventuality presented itself. He climbed into his Cherokee a few minutes before Noon and drove to the Paseo and around to Alameda Street. This time he turned right on Cathedral Place and parked at a meter.

Fernando crossed the street from the Saint Francis Cathedral to the La Fonda Hotel. He entered through the eastern side door and walked down a long hallway to the lobby, ignoring the display cases filled with glitzy jewelry and other Southwestern items for sale in the gift shops. Once in the lobby he looked away from the front counter, trying not to be noticed. He especially didn't want Fred Mondragon, the hotel manager, to spot him. Fred had blacklisted Fernando after a recent incident that really wasn't Fernando's fault.

The fateful event occurred this past spring when Fred had thrown out Fernando along with his friend Antonio Blake and Jack Lacy, known to law enforcement as the Santa Fe Assassin. The three of them had made quite a scene, after Lacy went ballistic while eating lunch on La Plazuela. Lacy bolted up from the table, knocking over his chair and yelling that he'd seen a ghost. Embarrassing didn't begin to describe the horror of that incident, with chairs falling and Lacy shouting and security guards rushing over to escort them off the premises while everyone on La Plazuela stared at them in disbelief as if they were lunatics. Fred just shook his head from across the way at the front counter. Whatever happened today, Fernando did not want a repeat of that scene with Tom Doering.

Like it or not, Fernando had acquired a bad reputation in the shops and hotels in downtown Santa Fe. Trouble just seemed to follow him everywhere, like a damn shadow. Sometimes Fernando felt cursed, actually cursed, like someone somewhere had a voodoo doll in his image and was constantly jabbing it—him—with pins. He didn't necessarily believe in curses or voodoo, but he did know for a fact that people with problems always seemed to find him.

Fernando ducked down and used a group of tourists as a shield as he walked across the lobby. When he spotted Tom Doering, his spirits sank. Doering sat next to another man with a similar pale, pudgy face. But unlike Doering's button-down business look, this fellow wore sweat pants and a Nike exercise shirt and looked like he had the muscles to support it.

Sighing, Fernando walked to their table in the middle of La Plazuela and took a seat across the table from the two of them, who could have been brothers, maybe even twins.

"I brought my man Roy with me," Doering said.

Once again Fernando didn't like the implied threat. "What do you mean by your 'man'? Is he your twin brother? Your yoga instructor? What?"

Doering shot a glance at Roy. He looked nervous, trying to get comfortable in his chair. He cleared his throat and said, "He helps out. When I need it."

"Yeah, I brought some help too," Fernando countered, motioning toward his Smith & Wesson.

Roy remained expressionless, saying nothing.

"So what do you want to talk about, Doering?" Fernando asked, losing his patience. He wanted to get out of here before Fred noticed him. He desperately wanted to avoid another scene.

Doering fidgeted with his menu on the table. "Well, Athena has reconsidered her offer. She's willing to pay you fifty thousand dollars to walk away. You don't have to do anything, just walk away and let the situation play out. As simple as that. She just wants to sell the gallery and be done with it. Surely you can understand that."

"As simple as that?"

"As simple as that," Doering repeated. "No questions asked."

"Sorry, but I do have a question," Fernando said. "Just what are you trying to hide? People like you and Athena don't give away money and not expect to get something in return. What is it?"

"I told you, she wants a quick sale."

"You keep saying that, but what does my investigation have to do with a quick sale?" Fernando asked. "Why do you want me to stop? You must be afraid I'll find whatever it is you're trying to hide. So why don't you just tell me and let me decide what to do? What are you hiding?"

Doering's mouth tightened. He was angry now. "Listen, I'm giving you a chance to make fifty thousand dollars for keeping your mouth shut. What more could you possibly want?"

"For keeping my mouth shut about what? That's what I want to know," Fernando said.

Suddenly Doering lost his temper and slammed his closed fist down on the table, rattling the silverware and startling the other diners, all of whom stared at them. One woman yelped.

Here we go again, Fernando thought. Helpless, he could do nothing but watch the incident unfold in front of him. He knew he would regret what was about to happen next. As would Fred Mondragon.

Roy quickly reached over and grabbed Doering's arm, trying to calm him before he did something stupid. Too late.

"Look...we know where you live...where your wife works," Doering said with clenched teeth. "We'll..."

Doering never finished his sentence.

Fernando reacted instinctively at the mention of his wife. He shoved the table hard into Doering's gut, hearing the pale man from Cincinnati yelp. Roy tried to jump up from the table but stumbled and fell backward on his chair. The crash echoed loudly off the walls of La Plazuela.

Fernando pointed to Doering. "If you lay a hand on my wife, I'll kill you. If you even come close to her, I'll kill you!"

Doering sputtered, too angry to speak. He grabbed his abdomen with both hands and moaned.

Fernando stood up and looked down at Roy, struggling on all fours now trying to get to his feet. "The same goes for you," he said to Roy.

Fernando turned and walked away. He brushed past a couple of servers who stood in his way watching the fracas with open mouths, frozen in place as if they didn't know whether to continue working or flee. Once past the servers Fernando marched out of La Plazuela into the lobby.

Unfortunately Fred Mondragon had been watching everything from the front counter. Looking as dapper as always in his tan suit and white tie, Fred threw open his arms wide. "What the fuck, Fernando?" the usually proper man asked, unable to control himself.

"Sorry, Fred," Fernando said as he walked by the counter. "Maybe you should do a better job of screening your clientele."

Furious, Fernando walked down the hall and exited through the side door. He crossed Cathedral Place, climbed into his Cherokee, and hit the ignition. Then he changed his mind and killed the ignition. Instead, he sat in the driver's seat brooding. Doering's threats against Estelle changed everything. Now it was personal, as well as more complicated. He couldn't ask Estelle to go stay with their daughter Flavia in Tesuque. Not again. He'd already sent her to Flavia's once this year during the Pecos case, when the man they called the Foreman showed up in Santa Fe hunting the cops who sent him to prison, including Fernando.

Back then Estelle had told him in no uncertain terms that she would never 'hide out' again, ever. That he was retired and had no business getting involved in criminal cases involving murderers. And that if he ever asked her to leave again, however briefly, she would up and leave him permanently. Period!

They'd had their share of arguments in the past, but he'd never seen Estelle this angry. He believed her now. He had no reason to doubt that she would carry out her threat.

So what to do? All of his options were bad. If he dared to explain the situation to Estelle, there was no telling what she would do. If he said nothing, he would put her in harms way.

Finally he gave up. He couldn't see a path forward, so he started the Cherokee and drove back to the Paseo and around to Acequia Madre. His house no longer felt safe after his run-in with Doering. He pulled into the driveway and parked close to the house, just in case he needed to leave quickly.

Once inside he went directly to his study and took his Steyr sniper rifle down from the closet shelf. He loaded the rifle and placed it behind the door of his study out of sight where it would be convenient to grab, if he needed it quickly. Then he checked all the windows and the side door that looked out on a dense thicket of bushes along Acequia Madre

Street to make sure everything was locked and connected to their security system. They only used the security system when they went out of town for a day or more, but tonight he would activate the system before going to bed. He didn't know what else he could do.

When finished, he sat at the kitchen table and waited for Estelle to come home from work. About five o'clock he heard her Camry pull into their driveway and park by their garage. He dreaded what was about to happen. A few moments later the kitchen door opened and Estelle walked into the kitchen carrying her purse and the white canvas bag she used to transport things back and forth from home to her work at the outreach program.

Estelle stopped. "What's wrong with you?" she asked, noticing that something was awry.

"Pull up a chair, I need to tell you something," Fernando said.

1 6

Fernando awoke from someone shaking him. He opened his eyes a crack and saw Estelle hovering over him. Was she trying to choke him to death after their conversation last night? It hadn't gone well. She'd once again warned him that he would have to choose between her and his new calling as a fixer, whatever that was. Detective, private investigator, fixer, what difference did it make? Estelle asked. She said it didn't matter what he called himself—it brought the same trouble down on both of them. And she was finished with it. No more trouble.

"Your cell phone has been ringing," Estelle said. "I'm just about to leave for work."

He waited a few moments to get his wits about him and then climbed out of bed slowly. After visiting the master bath, he pulled on his jeans and a clean work shirt from his closet and headed for the kitchen. There on the kitchen table he found Estelle's epistle. Scribbled in big black letters on a piece of legal size paper he read: "You make a decision, fast!"

Last night she'd refused point blank to stay with Flavia for even one day. She blamed him for getting himself—and her—in one dangerous situation after another. On and on for about an hour, a real tongue-lashing. He'd only seen Estelle that angry once before: when she found out about his one-weekend affair with Linda, the day dispatcher down at the Washington Avenue Station.

He knew Estelle was right. He had to stop taking these cases, if you could call them cases. There was no reason to continue. He wasn't even being paid for what he was doing. He swore to himself that he would never do this again...once he finished the Sonny Davis case.

Fernando scrounged around in the refrigerator looking for something to eat that he wouldn't have to cook. He found an old chicken enchilada with red sauce, which he loved, so he wolfed that down standing at the sink and then grabbed a croissant and cup of coffee and headed out to the patio. More and more the patio had become his place of refuge. When he felt agitated, the serenity of the cottonwoods and aspens along Acequia Madre Street quieted him. Same when he felt himself going to the dark place. The sight of the adobe walls, sprinkled with sunflowers and blue and red hollyhocks, always improved his mood.

He finished his cup of coffee and went inside to get another. When he returned he found his cell phone ringing on the bench.

"Lopez," he answered.

"Mister Lopez, I'm sorry, I didn't know who to call," a vaguely familiar woman's voice on the other end said. He couldn't quite place her.

"Who is this?"

"It's Mary Margaret, I'm sorry," the voice said. "I'm calling because Becca is missing...and I don't know what to do. She didn't show up for work again today. I keep calling, but she doesn't answer her phone. I'm worried that something terrible has happened to her."

"Why do you think something terrible has happened to her? Maybe she just went out of town for a day or so and forgot to tell you. Up to Taos or Abiquiu, maybe," Fernando said.

When Mary Margaret didn't respond, Fernando asked, "Well, have you filed a missing persons report with the police?"

"No, not yet. I don't know if I want to get the police involved."

Fernando hesitated before responding. He didn't know what she expected him to say or do.

"I didn't know who to call, but I remembered you seemed interested in helping us," Mary Margaret said. "I can't talk with Athena, because she and Becca had a terrible argument the other day."

"No kidding," Fernando said, getting interested now. "What was the argument about?"

"Maybe Becca's absences, I don't really know."

"Okay, but how can I help?" Fernando asked, regretting his offer as soon as he'd made it.

"I'm on my way to Becca's apartment right now," Mary Margaret said. "Her landlord's gonna meet me there and let me in. Could you come along? I'm a little scared to go by myself."

Fernando had no idea why she was scared to go by herself, but he said, "Okay. Where is it?"

"Number ten in the Fort Marcy Apartments," Mary Margaret said. "Right across from Fort Marcy Park."

"I'll meet you there," Fernando said and clicked off.

He was familiar with Fort Marcy Apartments—an old, slightly rundown complex that resembled a two-story Marriott Residence Inn without the charm. Fort Marcy Apartments catered to younger, less-affluent renters than most other apartments in Santa Fe. During his years as a police detective he'd been called there on several occasions, most involving domestic abuse complaints or drug-related issues. A bit shady, that's how he remembered the place.

Just like that, Fernando forgot his new resolution to avoid trouble.

Fernando set the security alarm and locked the house. He carried his Smith & Wesson to the Cherokee and locked it in the glove compartment, where it would be in the odd chance he needed it at Fort Marcy Apartments. Then he drove down to the Paseo and around to Bishop's Lodge Road. Once past the turn-off to Hyde Park Road, Fort Marcy Apartments came into view. It looked to him like the apartments had been spiffed up since the last time he was here. The units had been newly painted and the landscape gardening had been improved with the addition of bright flowers and bushes all around the compound.

Fernando pulled up in front of Number 10, one of the units on the lower level of the frame and stucco building. Wooden stairways led to the rooms on the upper level. The door to Number 10 stood wide open. Inside he saw two people talking. One of them was Mary Margaret; he could tell by her blond hair. The other was a bald, middle aged man with a noticeable stoop who he'd never seen before. The Fort Marcy Apartments landlord, he assumed.

Fernando walked up to the porch and stepped through the open door into a tiny studio apartment: a small front room, an open kitchen, one bedroom and what looked like a small bath in back. Mary Margaret and the bald man had moved into the kitchen, where they stood glancing at him over the counter. Mary Margaret pointed to Fernando and waved.

"Mister Lopez, thanks for coming," Mary Margaret said, wearing a short, tight dress more appropriate for a cocktail party than work. She motioned toward her companion. "This is Stan Pearlman, Becca's landlord. I told him you might come to help out."

Pearlman waved.

"Howdy," Fernando said and walked through the front room, seeing nothing amiss, no overturned furniture or anything that would indicate a kidnapping had occurred here. He stopped at the kitchen counter, looking across at Mary Margaret and Pearlman on the other side.

"Like I was just saying, I don't want any trouble," Pearlman said to Fernando. "I don't know anything about Miss Thomas' whereabouts. She always pays her rent on time, and she seems like a very nice young lady. That's really all I know about her. Sorry, I can't be more helpful."

Fernando nodded. Looking around the small unit, he said, "I don't see any evidence of a kidnapping or any violence occurring here. There must be another explanation."

"But what?" Mary Margaret asked. "Becca and I are best friends. She couldn't have just disappeared without telling me."

Pearlman raised his hand. "Well...I'll let the two of you sort things out. Just close the door when you leave. The door will lock automatically." With that, he walked out of the apartment, leaving the front door open.

Fernando waited until Pearlman had gone before saying, "Check the bedroom. Look for any evidence that Becca packed an overnight bag or a suitcase, some indication that she'd left on a trip or maybe just an overnight getaway."

While Mary Margaret checked the bedroom, Fernando walked into the kitchen and found clean, tidy counters. Everything had been put away neatly in the cupboards. No dirty dishes or food left out. Even the trash can was empty. Again he saw no indication of foul play.

He moved over to the refrigerator and opened the door. The refrigerator wasn't very well stocked, lots of yogurt and cheese and a container of milk, but not much else. That wasn't unusual for a young person of Becca's age. Like most young people, she probably didn't do much cooking. Most likely she ate most of her meals out, except breakfast.

Closing the door he noticed a calendar attached to the side of the refrigerator by magnets. He looked closely and found Wednesday of last week circled and OB-GYN written in the circle. Otherwise the calendar was free of entries.

"Yes!" he heard Mary Margaret say from the bedroom.

Fernando left the kitchen and joined Mary Margaret in the bedroom. He saw a scattering of clothes tossed on the double bed in the center of the room, everything from underwear to tights and light sweaters.

Mary Margaret pointed to a suitcase on the floor of the bedroom closet. "See, her large suitcase is still here, but the small carry-on Becca always uses for short trips is missing."

Fernando nodded, still looking at the clothes on Becca's bed. "Looks like she went through her clothes to choose what to take with her. The smaller the suitcase, the more picky you have to be."

"Yeah, well, I don't get it," Mary Margaret said. "She must have gone somewhere, but why wouldn't she tell Angelica and I? We have to cover for her when she doesn't come in for work. The three of us are like sisters. We tell each other everything, and we cover for each other."

"But you said earlier that she'd been missing a lot of work," Fernando reminded Mary Margaret. "Just not showing up."

"True...I don't know what's gotten into her lately."

Fernando closed the door of the closet and turned back to Mary Margaret. "That's the question. Has she mentioned anything about a vacation? Some sort of local getaway maybe?"

Mary Margaret shook her head. "Not a word."

Fernando looked around the room again and then back to Mary Margaret. "Does she have a boyfriend, someone she likes to do things with on the spur of the moment? Go up to Taos or Abiquiu maybe?"

"No, she broke up with her boyfriend earlier this year. I think it was because of her relationship with Sonny," Mary Margaret said, frowning. "The boyfriend didn't approve of it."

Fernando laughed. "I can imagine."

Mary Margaret blushed.

Not knowing what to think, Fernando looked around again. Finally he asked, "What if someone forced her to come with them? You know, forced her to pack a bag and whatever she would need before leaving. Does Becca have any enemies that you're aware of? Someone who might want to force her to come with them? A jealous boyfriend from the past, for example. Someone she quarreled with maybe? Or a family member angry about what was happening at work and wanting to save her from being sexually assaulted by Sonny?"

Mary Margaret shrugged. "No, not that I know of, except I told you about the arguments she was having with Athena. I suppose because of all the days she's missed at work. She just didn't show up, didn't even call."

"Hmmm...did Athena's brother Tom participate in these arguments?" Fernando asked.

"No, but he watched," she said. "He was there, he just didn't say much. He's like that, he lets Athena make all the decisions."

Fernando looked around one last time. "Well, if I were you, I would report this to the police as a missing person. It's been over twenty four hours, so the police will take it seriously."

Mary Margaret frowned. "Oh my God, what if she's dead in a ditch somewhere....?"

Her question lingered in the stale air of the small apartment, a long moment of silence.

Finally Fernando said, "Well, let's don't get ahead of ourselves," the only words of comfort he had to offer.

17

Fernando walked out of Becca's apartment first and waited for Mary Margaret to close the door. Then he made sure the door locked securely, not wanting to leave it unsecured for possible intruders. The moment he stepped off the porch he saw the silver Mercedes at the entrance of the driveway to the apartment compound, waiting. Tom Doering and his stooge Roy.

"What do they want?" Mary Margaret asked behind him.

Fernando could feel his blood pressure spiking. The anger over feeling like a hunted animal returned with a vengeance. He quickly turned to Mary Margaret and barked, "Listen...go directly to your car and get out of here as fast as you can. I'll take care of this."

Without speaking, she did as she was told. She hurried to her car, a gray Nissan Rogue, and did not even glance at the Mercedes. Once inside she locked the doors and started the engine. Then she waved.

Fernando stood watching. Mary Margaret's gray Nissan drove past the Mercedes and turned left on Bishop's Lodge Road. It quickly disappeared over a small rise heading back toward Santa Fe. The Mercedes didn't follow.

Not knowing what to expect, Fernando went directly to the Cherokee and unlocked the glove compartment. He took his time now, breathing deeply and trying to relax. Resigned, he strapped on the open-carry holster holding his Smith & Wesson. It was show time.

Fernando marched across the parking lot to the Mercedes. He stopped at the driver's side window and knocked on the glass with his knuckles. The window opened revealing Tom Doering at the wheel. Roy sat in the passenger's seat, riding shotgun. Both men stared at him, silent. As if they were sorely disappointed to find him here and wanted Fernando to know it.

"Becca's missing," Fernando said, standing back from the window and holding on tight to his Smith & Wesson.

Doering shook his head. "No...she's with Athena. They're at a staff retreat. We were on our way there now when we saw your car."

"Staff retreat? Then why isn't Mary Margaret there?"

"I don't know. She wasn't invited, I suppose."

Skeptical, Fernando said, "In a retreat you bring all your employees together to discuss issues and then come to solutions. You don't invite one person and call it a staff retreat."

"Whatever you say," Doering said, starting the Mercedes. Then he pointed to Fernando and said, "We're watching you."

With that Doering rolled up the window. He made a U-turn and then shot off fast down Bishop's Lodge Road, heading west toward Bishop's Lodge Resort and the village of Tesuque. Not back to Santa Fe.

Fernando watched them disappear over a small rise, still clutching his Smith & Wesson.

Finally Fernando walked over to his Cherokee, where he removed his holster and put it back in the glove compartment. What a way to start the day. He'd barely had enough coffee before Mary Margaret called. Time to start over and hope for a better result.

He pulled out of the parking lot and drove slowly back into Santa Fe, troubled by Doering's comment about a retreat. Bullshit, no doubt about it. But why would Athena be with Becca somewhere out in Tesuque? Something was missing. There was too much he didn't know about what was going on at Athena Gallery.

When he came to the Paseo, he turned left and headed home. Then he had second thoughts and instead turned left on Canyon Road and drove up to Athena Gallery. Mary Margaret's gray Nissan Rogue was parked on the side of the building in the employee lot, next to a small yellow Fiat, which Fernando supposed belonged to Angelica. He parked in front and walked through the front garden into the gallery. Angelica and Marry Margaret, who had just arrived, stood talking in whispers over by the counter. Both looked worried.

Fernando waved as he walked in. "I talked to Tom Doering after you left. He said Becca was with Athena at a staff retreat. Do either of you know anything about a staff retreat?"

"News to me," Angelica replied.

Mary Margaret laughed. "Nobody invited us. So if they are having a retreat, it must be a retreat for Becca. Sounds suspicious."

"I know," Fernando said, walking up to the counter. "You think they could be holding Becca against her will for some reason?"

"Becca's been absent a lot lately, but you can't hold someone prisoner for that, last time I checked," Angelica quipped. "Why wouldn't they just dock her if they're concerned with her absences? Or fire her?"

Mary Margaret shrugged. "I don't know, but we better get the computers up and running, so we can open. I don't want to end up in a retreat with the Doerings, or whatever they're doing with or to Becca."

"Okay, you have my card. Call me if you see Becca or learn anything about her whereabouts," Fernando said.

Even more troubled, Fernando left the gallery and climbed back into his Cherokee. He drove down to the Paseo and around to Acequia Madre and then turned into his driveway. When he entered the house, he went directly to his study and sat down with his laptop. He needed more information about Tom Doering. Physically, Doering didn't appear that dangerous, but he knew very well that appearances could be deceptive. Just how dangerous was this guy? Could he and Athena have been so bold as to kidnap Becca for her transgressions, whatever they were? He should have checked out Doering earlier.

With that in mind, Fernando booted up his laptop and googled 'Thomas Doering, Cincinnati Ohio.' Instantly a column of citations and news stories appeared on his screen. He saw immediately that Doering was an attorney practicing in Cincinnati, a tax attorney no less. He specialized in contesting audits and IRS decisions on behalf of large businesses and corporations. Hardly a surprise. He apparently made a handsome living chasing the big payday, according to everything he read online. Doering was also an arts patron and a longtime member of the Cincinnati Country Club. A man used to getting his way, as Athena had said.

On the other hand, Fernando found nothing on Roy, Doering's 'man,' whatever that meant: friend, driver, bodyguard? He wasn't listed on Doering's website as an employee. Roy looked a bit more dangerous than Doering, but not much. Closing the laptop, he went outside to their patio, where he did his best thinking. He sat in the usual spot on his bench and pondered his next move. If Doering was telling the truth about having a retreat, maybe bringing in the employees one at a time and then all together, they would need a place that would accommodate a retreat. Any of the large hotels in the area would have meeting rooms. But Doering drove off down Bishop's Lodge Road toward Tesuque. The only large hotel in Tesuque was Bishop's Lodge Resort unless they went all the way to Pojoaque, but the Pojoaque hotels were mostly casinos. A casino didn't strike him as a good place to hold a retreat. That left the one and only Bishop's Lodge Resort.

Fernando had to smile. It seemed every rich schmuck of dubious character wanting decadent luxury with total anonymity ended up at Bishop's Lodge Resort. Hadn't he just directed the assassin Jack Lacy there in his recent Santa Fe Assassin case and before him Belle Longstreet in his Painted Skull Ranch case? It was a good place to go off grid and still enjoy all the amenities, if you were a member of the over class and could afford the prices.

He knew Athena Gallery closed at five p.m., so he decided to set a trap. He would return to the Fort Marcy Apartments about 4:30 or so and wait in the parking lot until he saw either Tom or Athena driving by on Bishop's Lodge Road. Either Tom's silver Mercedes or Athena's white Lexus, it didn't matter which. Then he would follow one or both of them to Bishop's Lodge Resort or wherever they were heading. He would find them and confront them. To hell with the fifty thousand dollars Athena was offering him to back off.

Truth was, he'd taken a strong disliking to the Doering clan.

18

Fernando checked his watch. Quarter past five. He'd been waiting at Fort Marcy Apartments for over thirty minutes. He'd parked off to the side of the apartment complex, so the Cherokee would be all but invisible to motorists driving by on Bishop's Lodge Road. Always impatient, Fernando hated waiting. One of his many faults. Sitting in a hot vehicle just made the situation worse. He opened the driver's door, deciding to get out and stretch his legs, maybe walk around the parking lot while he waited. Anything to break the monotony.

Just as he opened the door he heard a car approaching. Moments later he spotted a white Lexus sedan coming down Bishop's Lodge Road. It looked like the one he'd seen the other day at Athena Gallery. When it drove by the apartments, he recognized the older woman with short gray hair in the driver's seat. All by her lonesome in the big sedan, Athena headed west toward Tesuque.

Fernando started the Cherokee and shot off after her. He kept a good distance between him and the Lexus, not wanting to give Athena any warning that he was following her.

Up ahead, Athena braked as she began the long descent into the outskirts of Tesuque. He had to slow down to an uncomfortable twenty miles per hour in order to stay behind her. At the bottom of the hill Athena turned right into the driveway of Bishop's Lodge Resort, as he expected.

Fernando was all too familiar with Bishop's Lodge Resort. The exclusive resort anchored the eastern edge of Tesuque, just down the hill from Santa Fe. The 400-acre property had an illustrious history, first purchased in the 1860s by Archbishop Jean Baptiste Lamy, the subject of Willa Cather's novel *Death Comes for the Archbishop*. Lamy built a chapel on the grounds and used it as a retreat. The lodge itself dated from the 1920s but in recent years had been remodeled and greatly expanded to accommodate what the owners referred to as the "luxury traveler," by which they meant the filthy rich. Rooms and casitas at the upscaled lodge could run upwards of one thousand dollars a night.

Fernando frowned as he turned into the long driveway. The proverbial money changers had entered the temple. Archbishop Lamy must be turning over in his dusty grave.

He followed the outer loop around to the Cottonwood Casita, which he remembered because both Belle Longstreet and Jack Lacy had stayed there. Athena, however, drove past the Cottonwood Casita and parked her Lexus in front of the next unit down, the Sunset Cottage. Tom Doering's silver Mercedes was already parked between the Cottonwood Casita and the Sunset Cottage.

Fernando waited until Athena walked into the Sunset Cottage and then pulled up behind her Lexus. Leaving his Smith & Wesson in the locked glove compartment, he climbed out of his Cherokee and walked through an elaborate flower garden up to the veranda. Out of the corner of his eye he noticed two men approaching on the left. Both wore swimming trunks and carried towels, suggesting they were returning to the casita area from the pool. He didn't pay too much attention to the swimmers, but just as he reached for the front door one of them grabbed Fernando's collar from behind and pulled him backwards.

Turning, Fernando recognized the swimmers: Tom Doering and his stooge Roy. He should have known.

Instinctively Fernando jabbed his right elbow into his assailant's gut as hard as he could, with 180 pounds of muscle behind it. The man behind him groaned and then gasped for air. When Fernando spun around he saw Roy on his hands and knees retching on the sidewalk, while Tom kept his distance, a look of horror on his face. It was clear that Tommy boy was a money man, not a fighter.

Fernando pointed his trigger finger at Roy and said, "You touch me again and I'll really hurt you!"

Roy continued retching.

Fernando turned to Tom and flashed him an angry look. Tom

took a step back, without saying a word. Worried, he glanced to his left and then his right, as if looking for a way to escape.

With that Fernando pounded on the front door of the cottage and then said the hell with it and helped himself. He burst through the door, surprising Athena, who stood in the center of the front room with her mouth hanging open.

"Where is she?" Fernando demanded.

Athena tried to compose herself. "Becca? She...she's indisposed. She can't see visitors at the moment. This is not a good time."

"Where is she?" Fernando repeated, stepping up into her face and forcing Athena to back up. He glanced around the casita, plush with Southwestern décor throughout, everything from Navajo patterned upholstery on the furniture to kiva fireplaces in the corners and vigas on the ceilings. He saw a kitchen and two bedrooms off the front sitting room.

Ignoring Athena, Fernando marched back to the bedrooms. In the smaller of the two bedrooms he saw Becca sitting up in bed wearing loose cotton sweats with a lap blanket pulled up over her legs. Her matted hair and pale complexion made her look tired, maybe sick, as though she were in the middle of a long convalescence. But why? Something was terribly wrong here.

"Are you okay?" Fernando asked.

Becca nodded. "I'm getting better...they're taking care of me," she said weakly, struggling to get out from underneath her blanket. She seemed incredibly weak, nothing like the frisky young woman he'd seen earlier.

Athena came up alongside Fernando and touched his arm. She motioned for him to come back into the front sitting room to talk. "Please, let me explain," she said softly, almost a whisper.

Annoyed, Fernando hesitated a moment and then turned around and followed her into the front room.

"Becca had a medical abortion yesterday," Athena said, still whispering. "She's had the usual cramping and bleeding, nothing to worry about. She's a little tired right now is all. She'll feel better in a day or so."

"Medical abortion? You mean surgery?" Fernando asked.

"No, the abortion pill, misoprostol," Athena replied. "I know you men don't know much about it, only that you want to control our bodies, right?"

Fernando raised his hands. "No, I don't want to control anyone. I have a hard enough time controlling myself."

"Hmmm...whatever you say," Athena responded, not believing him.

"Was it successful?" Fernando asked.

Athena nodded. "Once again you can see the damage my ex-husband did to those around him. He got Becca pregnant and took no responsibility for the pregnancy. He was a reckless, unconscionable brute who ruined lives as easily as he ruined his body with alcohol and risky sex."

Fernando couldn't resist. "Is that why you killed him?"

"Wrong," Athena responded. "I was in Cincinnati when Sonny was killed. You know that."

He did know that, which is what made Sonny's murder such a mystery. Athena had the motive, but not the opportunity. Not surprisingly, her fingerprints were not on the murder weapon, whereas everyone else involved in the case had left their fingerprints smeared all over the Glock pistol.

"So you should leave," Athena said. "This is woman's business now. We have to clean up the messes you men make. I can't tell you how angry I get sometimes. I know it's not your fault. You seem like a decent man, but most of the men I've met, including Sonny and my first husband, were selfish, careless brutes."

Fernando had heard a version of this rant from Estelle and Linda and countless other women. He didn't need to hear it again from Athena. He turned and walked back into the bedroom.

Becca's eyes were half closed. She hadn't moved.

"Do you need my help?" Fernando asked. "Is there anything I can do for you before I leave?"

Becca smiled and opened her eyes. She shook her head.

Fernando motioned to his watch and then waved his hand in a circular motion, hoping to suggest that he would return later. Hopefully when the Doering clan was not here.

Then he turned and walked into the front sitting room.

"My offer is still good, by the way," Athena said, following him to the front door. "You'd be a fool not to take it."

"So I've heard," Fernando said.

With that, he flashed Athena a mock salute and stepped outside on the veranda. Tom Doering and Roy stood back and watched as he walked through the garden. Neither of them said a word.

Just the sight of them enraged Fernando. He walked right up to them and poked Doering hard in the chest. "If either of you clowns harms that young woman, you'll answer to me. It won't be pretty."

He wished Tom or Roy would take a step toward him. At the moment he wanted nothing more than to smash one of their pale, pudgy faces. No such luck. Chickenshits, both of them.

Fernando climbed into his Cherokee and slammed the door shut as loud as he could. Then he fired up the big engine and drove off, not a happy camper. Now what? On the way back to town he ran through the list of people whose fingerprints were on the murder weapon: Ruby, Tessa, Mary Margaret, Angelica, Becca, and Blaine who had stupidly brought the damn gun to Athena Gallery. That was downright ironic since Blaine had made such a big deal about Tessa moving the gun from Ruby's gallery to his gallery. One of them, or someone as yet unknown, pulled the trigger on that Glock pistol and killed Sonny. He had no interest in interrogating all of them again, especially Ruby and Tessa. Not to mention Blaine. They would just repeat the same bullshit stories they'd given him earlier.

When he came to the garish Scottish Rite Center, he turned left on the Paseo and took it around to Canyon Road. He was late for Happy Hour at El Farol.

Sonny Davis was already dead, so why did it matter who killed him?

Hadn't Athena said the same thing?

What possible difference would it make?

19

The moment Fernando stepped into El Farol he heard Blaine's loud voice. The big man stood over by the colorful Flamenco mural where the regulars always gathered. He was cursing the Santa Fe Police Department and waving his hands in the air wildly. He wore his usual red Bermuda shorts with a bright turquoise T-shirt today, the T-shirt referencing the Turquoise Trail that ran south of Santa Fe to the towns of Cerrillos and Madrid and then all the way to Albuquerque. Blaine looked like a demented circus clown with a bad temper.

"Awww, shut up and sit down, ya jackass," Ruby ordered. "Manny isn't going to arrest any of us. Don't be so hysterical."

"Hah!" Blaine responded. "The cops are looking for someone to pin Sonny's murder on. Tessa and I are the likely targets because she made the first mistake by bringing the gun over to my gallery. You might be okay because Manny's your friend, but he doesn't like me."

Tessa slammed her drink down on the table. "Here we go again with the blame Tessa crap."

Ruby ignored Tessa and instead turned her attention to Blaine. "No one likes you, Blaine, but that doesn't mean Manny will arrest you. All our fingerprints are on that gun every last one of us. And so what, we have Raoul Garcia defending us. Our lame-ass prosecutor Steve Chabot won't go up against Raoul, you know that..."

Blaine noticed Fernando approaching. He abruptly changed focus and started a new rant. "Oh shit, don't tell me you have more bad news. I can tell by that look on your face. What now?"

"Nice to see you, too," Fernando said, taking a seat next to Dave Stein, across the table from Ruby and Tessa.

Penny, one of the afternoon bartenders, almost beat Fernando to the table delivering his Modelo draft. All the bartenders and servers at El Farol knew what Fernando drank. "Thanks, Penny," he said.

Blaine gave him the Evil Eye. "Well? What's the story? Don't keep us in suspense, for Chrissake."

Fernando took a long drink of his Modelo and sighed. "Turns out our late friend Sonny not only sexually assaulted, but knocked up Becca. So yesterday Becca had an abortion. That's my news."

"That sonofabitch!" Ruby said angrily. "He preyed on those girls for years. He oughta been castrated."

Blaine shook his head. "Jesus, you'd think he would have used protection."

Ruby's face turned red. "That's all you have to say? What's wrong with you, Blaine?"

"No wonder everybody wanted to kill him," Tessa added.

"Yeah, and that's the problem," Fernando said. "Everybody wanted to kill him and everybody's fingerprints are on the murder weapon. Well, not everybody. I'm exaggerating, but you get the point."

While they talked Dave Stein fell asleep and started to snore, his chin resting on his chest.

Fernando turned to look at Sleeping Beauty. "Should I wake him up?"

"Nah, let him sleep," Ruby said. "He'll wake up when we leave. Otherwise they'll wake him up when they need the room for dinner."

Before long Blaine and Tessa said goodbye and made their way out of El Farol, arms around each other's waist, lovey-dovey again. One minute they were yelling at each other, the next minute they were smooching.

Ruby took the opportunity to move closer to Fernando. "So what's the scoop? Tell me more about Becca's abortion."

"I don't know much more than that," Fernando replied. "She had a medical abortion yesterday—the pill, not surgery. Then, for some reason, maybe because she feels in some ways responsible, Athena put her up at a cottage at Bishop's Lodge Resort where she's resting and recovering. Athena said Becca has cramps and bleeding, but nothing unusual. Becca seemed okay, although she was in bed when I got there and very weak. She said Athena was taking good care of her, whatever that means. That's pretty much all I know."

"Hmmm...I wonder," Ruby said.

"Wonder what?" Fernando asked.

"Why Athena's going to all that trouble and expense to nurse Becca," Ruby said. "Just because her ex-husband knocked her up? I don't buy that. Something's going on here that we don't know."

"Maybe she feels guilty that Sonny got her pregnant."

"Hah! That's a laugh," Ruby said. "Athena's a cold-blooded business woman. I doubt she's ever felt a sense of guilt in her entire life. Must be something more devious than that. Maybe she's trying to keep Becca quiet. More to the point, maybe she's trying to keep Becca from suing."

"Yeah, maybe," Fernando said, thinking the same thing, now that Ruby had mentioned it.

"One thing for sure, all this would give Athena another reason to want Sonny dead and gone," Ruby continued. "You understand what I'm saying, mister private detective?"

Fernando understood all too well. "I do, but Athena didn't arrive in Santa Fe until after Sonny's murder. Same for her brother Tom and the guy Tom brought with him, Roy something."

Ruby shook her head. "You don't get it. Athena is a very devious woman. Trust me."

"What do you mean? Get what?" Fernando asked.

"Trust me," was all Ruby said.

20

Fernando awoke from a fitful sleep, tormented by what Ruby had said about Athena. She'd called Athena a cold-blooded, devious woman. No doubt. One thing for certain, as Ruby pointed out, Athena was the one person with the most to gain from Sonny's death. She even tried to sell the gallery out from under Sonny, even though legally he had the majority stake. They'd fought bitterly over the right to sell the gallery. Both wanted to take the money and run. The only way Athena could get what she wanted—a quick sale—was to get rid of Sonny. But how? Is that why she brought along her brother Tom and his friend Roy? Maybe the two of them had arrived in Santa Fe earlier than Athena to arrange the killing. Or maybe they arranged it from back in Cincinnati. It wasn't hard to find a hired killer if you had money and connections. He knew that now, after his recent experience with Jack Lacy, the so-called Santa Fe Assassin, who arrived in Santa Fe on a contract to kill a government official.

He fumbled for the clock on his night table. Past nine o'clock already. He hated to sleep this late because it always left him groggy. He crawled out of bed and washed his face in the master bath. Then he shuffled down the hall barefoot to the kitchen and checked the pot of coffee Estelle had left for him on her way to work. Cold as a day-old corpse. So he brewed himself a cup of Sumatra in his Keurig and headed outside before realizing he hadn't dressed. He took one look at his underwear and bare feet and then headed back to the bedroom to dress. Once he had jeans and boots on, he retraced his steps to the kitchen and took his coffee outside to the patio.

Sitting on his favorite bench, he drank the coffee slowly, gradually starting to wake up. When he finished, he returned to the kitchen and made himself a second cup of coffee, which he drank quickly in the kitchen. After that he went back to the bedroom and finished getting dressed. Given the time, he decided to skip breakfast. So he grabbed a croissant and ate it in the Cherokee while driving down to the Paseo and around to Canyon Road. On automatic pilot, he cruised up to his office. He parked and walked down the gravel path to his office door and fumbled with his keys. The office key was missing from his key chain. What the...?

"Fernando? What are you doing down there?" Ruby called out to him from the porch of her gallery next door. She looked concerned.

"I can't find my key," Fernando shouted back.

"Awww, Jesus, Mary, and Joseph, what now?" Ruby said, and went back inside her gallery. A moment later she reappeared with a key in her hand and marched down to his office to join him.

"Here," she said, handing Fernando the key. "You retired and closed your office, remember?"

Suddenly it hit him, why he didn't have the key. He'd retired and given the key back to Ruby, his landlord. He'd had a senior moment.

"Are you okay? Have you had a stroke or something?" Ruby asked, looking at him closely.

Fernando shook his head. "No, I think I'm okay. Just groggy this morning. I had a rough night."

Ruby continued to stare at him, not convinced. "Well...go on in. I kept the office just the way you left it, let me show you."

Fernando opened the door and stepped inside. Like Ruby said, the office was exactly the way he'd left it. He found his desk and office chair, his file cabinet, and two small chairs facing the desk. Even his mini-refrigerator remained.

"Welcome back," Ruby said. "Keep the key. Bring whatever you want down here. You can use the office for as long as you want. Be like old times. I miss having you next door. Gives me peace of mind knowing I have some security down here, not to mention a friendly shoulder to cry on when I need it."

"Thanks, Ruby," Fernando said.

He watched Ruby walk back to her gallery before closing the door behind him. He had no idea what he was doing here. Every morning like clockwork he got out of bed and, after finishing his coffee, headed out to the Cherokee intending to drive down to his office on Canyon Road. Sometimes he even made it into the driver's seat before realizing that he had retired and closed his office. Today he'd made it all the way down without remembering. He was now on automatic pilot, unable to shake the habit. Truth was, he hadn't been able to accept being retired. In retiring he'd lost his identity. Or had he? The work he'd been taking on as a fixer was just as rewarding, he told himself. He almost believed that.

Alone, Fernando opened all the windows to let in fresh air and then sat at his desk. It had been a long time, too long. He felt himself calming down now, his blood pressure dropping. Like getting oriented again to the place where he needed to be for his sanity. A place that felt like home.

Sitting at his desk, he continued to brood about Athena. He remembered when she'd hired him last year to get Sonny out of her life. He did what she asked, using just the right amount of physical persuasion to get Sonny to sign their divorce papers. But he suspected what she really wanted was for him to eliminate Sonny by whatever means necessary, so she could be done with him once and for all. Now she'd finally managed to get what she desired. A coincidence? He didn't believe in coincidence. He never had and never would.

Yes, it was true that everyone hated Sonny and even wished him dead, but none more so than his ex-wife Athena.

Not only that, but why would Athena put up Becca in expensive Bishop's Lodge Resort after her abortion? Wouldn't the normal reaction be to ostracize a younger woman who had an extra-marital affair with your husband, even if you hated the bastard? Certainly the normal reaction wouldn't be to treat the young interloper to an extravagantly expensive stay at a posh resort. It just didn't add up. Like Ruby said, something was missing. Something was going on here that they didn't understand. And the only way to find out required him to confront the people who would know, starting with Becca herself.

Feeling better now that he had some sense of direction, Fernando got up and walked around the office. A little dust, but nothing that would keep him from using the office. He didn't need to bring everything back, just his laptop. He could come down whenever he was working on a case, or whenever he just wanted to socialize with Ruby and the Canyon Road crowd.

Before leaving he opened the mini-frig and found it empty. So the only other thing he would have to bring down was a supply of Modelo and bottled water. He liked to keep both beer and water handy for when he needed them.

Finished surveying the premises, he closed all the windows he'd opened and then locked up his old and now new office and went next door to treat Ruby to lunch at El Farol.

21

" Thanks for lunch," Ruby said to Fernando as they left El Farol. "See, I knew it'd be useful to have you back."

"My pleasure, it's the least I can do," Fernando replied.

"Are you going to put up another sign?" Ruby asked.

"No, now that I call myself a fixer, I think I'll keep my work on the down low," Fernando said. "Off grid, if you know what I mean."

"I guess," Ruby said. "But how will you ever get customers?"

Fernando laughed. "Apparently I don't have to worry about that. Customers keep finding me with their problems, it's an endless stream. I'm serious. I've had nonstop requests from people who need me to fix their fuck-ups. Lots of people need help cleaning up their messes. So they call me. They get my name from Manny or Raoul or any of the people who knew me during my thirty years at the Santa Fe Police. They find me one way or another."

"Yeah, you don't need to tell me about it," Ruby responded. "Just looking at Tessa and Blaine and all the other assholes around here, I can understand their need to find someone to fix the messes they make but can't seem to fix themselves. Hey, but just keep it legal, okay. You don't want to end up down at the station on the other side of the law."

"Yes ma'am," Fernando said, as they walked up Canyon Road into the parking lot of Ruby's gallery. He climbed into his Cherokee and pulled out of the parking lot, waving to Ruby.

Suddenly determined, and tired of getting the runaround, Fernando drove down Canyon Road to the Paseo and around to Bishop's Lodge Road, where he turned right heading for the resort. He wanted some answers. Now.

Just before Tesuque Fernando turned right into the long drive to Bishop's Lodge Resort. He followed the loop around to Cottonwood Casita. From there he could see Tom Doering's silver Mercedes parked in front of Sunset Cottage. He saw no sign of Athena's white Lexus. Since he didn't want to confront Doering just yet, he parked on the far side of the Cottonwood Casita, out of sight. Then he walked over toward the stables, where he found a wooden bench in the shade from where he had a clear view of Sunset Cottage. From here he would wait until Doering left the cottage. He wanted to get Becca all by her lonesome.

So began the all-too-familiar waiting game, a game he hated with a passion. Waiting drove him crazy. He had to be active, doing something, didn't matter what. After half an hour he began to get restless, agitated. For relief he walked to the stables and spent a few minutes watching the workers bringing in hay and saddling horses for those resort guests who enjoyed riding. One of the workers noticed him watching and waved, thinking he was a guest. Fernando waved back. What the hell. Might as well be friendly to the workers.

He watched the horses for another thirty minutes or so before getting bored and deciding to move on. After touring the swimming pool area, he headed back to his bench by Sunset Cottage. At the bench he noticed the silver Mercedes backing out of the parking area next to the cottage. He watched while the Mercedes drove off down the loop heading toward the main entrance, where it turned left heading back to Santa Fe. Finally the coast was clear.

Fernando decided to leave his Cherokee where it was, just in case Tom or Athena reappeared. So he walked down to Sunset Cottage and stepped up to the door, debating whether to knock or just walk in. He decided on the latter, opening the door and walking into the empty front room. In fact, he saw no one in the casita as he walked through the rooms. Then he saw Becca outside on the private patio. Dressed in a bikini top and sweatpants, she wore dark sunglasses and a floppy straw hat while reclining on a chaise lounge. She looked relaxed and not nearly as tired as before, maybe the perfect time to question her. He hoped.

Fernando opened the wooden patio doors and stepped outside into the bright sunshine.

The noise startled Becca. "Mr. Lopez, what are you doing here?" she asked, not exactly happy to see him. She fidgeted with her bikini top, pushing it up so it completely covered her breasts.

"Hi Becca, I just wanted to ask you some follow-up questions while the Doerings weren't around," Fernando said, taking a seat on a nearby chaise without waiting for an invitation. "I get the sense that you can't talk freely in front of them. I hope you don't mind my intrusion."

"Well, I..."

Fernando cut her off. "I wondered how you ever got involved in all this...with Sonny."

Becca grimaced. She took a deep breath and then said, "Well, at first I thought Sonny was charming, what with his English accent and his clever sense of humor. I was only nineteen, you know. And he courted me every day, nonstop. At first it was just joking around and innocent touching or rubbing. He would come up behind me and touch me on the shoulder gently or sometimes give me a back rub, things like that. I thought it was perfectly normal for two people who worked closely together to be affectionate, or at least friendly. No harm, no foul, that sort of thing."

Becca sighed. "Then things got more complicated. Sonny started touching me in more private places and sometimes he tried to kiss me. At first I was put off, but after awhile it seemed sort of normal that our relationship would get more affectionate as we became better acquainted. Then I realized what he was doing with Angelica and Mary Margaret. I was incredibly naïve at the beginning, not knowing what was going on between them, but I happened to walk in one day after work to pick up a lunch bag and coffee mug I'd forgotten when I left work earlier. I found Sonny and Mary Margaret spread out on the Taos sofa in his office, both naked...."

"Having sex?"

"Yes, having sex," Becca said. "Sonny was crawling all over her from behind, with Mary Margaret on her hands and knees. I was shocked to find them doing that at work. I just sort of stood there looking at them with my mouth hanging open. Mary Margaret was moaning and Sonny started to howl when he saw me. They didn't even stop what they were doing. Sonny seemed to get more violent, pushing and shoving on Mary

Margaret while staring at me. Finally he stopped moving for a moment and asked, "Care to join us, baby?" Then he pushed in again and Mary Margaret screamed this time. That's when I turned and ran out of the gallery. After that I couldn't get that image out of my mind, the two of them naked on the Taos sofa having sex and screaming. I don't know. I started dreaming about Sonny, imagining me on that Taos sofa with him. I wasn't a virgin. I mean I'd had several boyfriends who liked to fool around, but I'd never had a sexual experience as intense as that. I wondered what it would be like. I was curious, I guess."

Fernando nodded, implying that he understood, even though he didn't understand. Not really.

"The very first time we had sex Sonny brought me flowers and asked me to stay after work. I knew what he intended to do. I was nervous all day waiting for it to happen. And a little scared too, but more than anything I wanted to experience what I'd seen on the Taos sofa, that passion. And it was as good as I'd hoped, that first time. Sonny was a great lover, even though he was a little rough. Every time we had sex after that he would get a little rougher, biting and hurting me. I didn't like it, but he expected me to perform just like his other girls, as he called us. After that the three of us, Mary Margaret and Angelica and I, became kind of like sisters. We would compare stories and take care of each other. I knew it was wrong, but I couldn't stop because all of us were doing it and, I'll admit, enjoying it. At least at the beginning."

Fernando raised his hand to stop her. "Did he pay you for sex?"

Becca shook her head. "No, we weren't hookers!" Becca responded, with a flash of anger. "I can't really explain. It just became part of the job, what was expected. And Sonny gave us gifts and bought us nice things. Sometimes he would take us to the Compound or another of the fancy restaurants in town. He treated us like we were his mistresses, all three of us."

Here Becca stopped for a moment. She removed her sunglasses and dried her eyes with a tissue before continuing. "Then everything changed," she said, suddenly looking sullen. She turned away from Fernando and looked out toward the green hills that surrounded Bishop's Lodge Resort, a pastoral scene of peace and tranquility and natural beauty.

"How? What do you mean?" Fernando asked.

Becca shook her head. "I found out I was pregnant. At first I was kind of excited. I thought I might want to keep the baby, kind of like the baby would be a collective infant that all four of us created. I know that sounds crazy, but we were almost like a family. Or so it seemed to me at the time. Hah! I was so naïve!"

Fernando held his tongue.

After pausing for a few moments, Becca continued. "Sonny, of course, laughed when I told him about my plan. He had absolutely no interest in children. You wouldn't believe what he said to me. I still can't believe it, after all the times we'd been together and all the gifts he'd given me. He said, 'Too bad you're not one of my dogs—I could have had you spayed earlier.' That did it. That was when I broke from him. To say that to a young girl...."

Tears trickled down from under Becca's sunglasses. She paused again to wipe her eyes. "I probably shouldn't be telling you all this. Athena told me not to tell anyone, you or the police."

"No, it's okay," Fernando said. "It stops with me. I'm not about to tell anyone else."

Becca nodded. "Athena was furious when she found out. She and Sonny had their worst shouting match ever. She slapped him and then he shoved her into the wall of the gallery. Afterwards she came up to me and told me to get an abortion. More like she demanded that I get an abortion. She promised to pay for it and put me up here until I recovered. At that time I didn't know whether I would have a medical or a surgical abortion, which is expensive, so I agreed."

"Yeah, I bet she wanted you to have an abortion. Didn't want any paternity test or lawsuits against her precious estate."

Becca gave him a cold look. "I suppose."

"So that's why you killed Sonny," Fernando said, as gently as possible. "I can understand that."

"No! It wasn't me!" Becca shot back. "It was Athena who wanted him dead."

"Athena?"

"Of course," she insisted.

Fernando nodded, not taking his eyes off Becca. He believed her.

Sort of. "Tell me the truth, are you being held here against your will? If so, I can get you out of here. Right now, if you want."

"Not exactly held, though Athena told me she wanted me to stay here for a while," Becca said. "She didn't say how long."

"Do you want to leave?"

Becca hesitated. "It is kind of lonely here. I guess I could stay with my parents. I haven't told them about the abortion. I haven't decided if I'm going to tell them. It would just upset them."

"You want to leave right now?" Fernando asked, hoping she would say yes so he could get her out of harm's way. There was no way to tell what Athena and her brother were capable of doing in order to protect themselves. "I'm serious. I can drop you off at your parents house right now."

She shook her head. "No, because I need to get my things together. Tomorrow I'll be stronger. They usually come about ten o'clock. If you come earlier, maybe eight or eight thirty, I'll have my things packed and be ready to go."

"Okay, that sounds like a good plan," Fernando said. "I'll be here before eight thirty. You be ready to go."

With that, Fernando pushed himself up out of the chaise. So as not to be seen, he exited through the patio gate and walked around behind the cottage to the parking area next to the Cottonwood Casita. Looked like the coast was clear, so he climbed into his Cherokee and drove off down the loop to the main entrance, where he turned left and headed back to Santa Fe.

On the drive back Fernando brooded about how and where he was going to confront Athena and her brother. Then he started worrying about how Estelle would react if she found out he'd reopened, sort of, his office. Had he reopened his office? He wasn't sure if this was something he really wanted to do or just a passing fantasy driven by boredom or nostalgia or some equally deep emotion he didn't understand and couldn't control.

One thing for sure, he didn't plan on telling Estelle about what had been happening at Athena gallery between Sonny and his three 'girls'. What she didn't know wouldn't piss her off.

22

Next morning Fernando was the first to rise, a rarity in their household. He quietly slipped out of the bed, leaving Estelle sound asleep, and then dressed and tip-toed down the hall to the kitchen. Trying not to make any noise, he made their morning coffee and scrambled some eggs for breakfast. He'd just sat down at the table to eat when Estelle came shuffling into the kitchen wearing her fuzzy robe and L.L. Bean slippers. She looked groggy and suspicious.

"Why are you up so early?" she asked, her eyes sleepy and her hair sticking up in wild disarray.

"Busy morning," Fernando replied. "I made coffee and scrambled eggs. Can I serve you some?"

"Just coffee, please. I'm still half asleep."

Fernando poured her a cup of coffee and set it on the table. He hadn't told her about his office and didn't plan to tell her today. Not until he had a better idea of just what he intended to do. If, that is, he ever figured out what he intended to do.

Estelle picked up the coffee cup but remained standing. She took a sip of the steaming black liquid. "Busy with what?"

Good question. It took Fernando a few seconds to decide how to answer. He couldn't easily or quickly explain that his morning plan was to kidnap the kidnapped Becca and then deliver her safe and sound to her parents' house in Santa Fe. That would require a whole lot of explanation, which he wanted to avoid. He didn't have time for another argument.

"I'm interviewing a suspect in the Sonny Davis murder," Fernando said, stretching the truth a bit.

"Why are you still working on that?" Estelle asked. "You don't have cases anymore. You're retired, remember?"

Fernando frowned. "I told you, I'm helping Ruby and Tessa. They think they might be charged with killing Sonny, so I'm trying to do what I can to find the actual killer to prevent that from happening."

Estelle gave him the Evil Eye but said nothing. Then she took her coffee and shuffled out of the kitchen back to the bedroom to get ready for work.

Fernando finished his breakfast. He left the remainder of the scrambled eggs and coffee for Estelle and then paused a moment. Did he want to take his Smith & Wesson? He decided to take it, just to be prepared if Tom and Roy were more dangerous than they looked. So he went into his study and took the holster out of his closet and then carried it outside to his Cherokee. He locked the pistol and holster in the glove compartment and then drove off down Acequia Madre. He turned right at the Paseo and took it around to Bishop's Lodge Road. Turning right onto Bishop's Lodge Road he checked the time. He'd told Becca he would arrive at the Sunset Cottage between eight and eight thirty, but the clock on the dash read 8:37. He was already late. He berated himself for not getting up earlier, as he had planned.

Fernando drove faster than he usually did, having to brake hard at the bottom of the hill into Tesuque. He swerved right and followed the loop into Bishop's Lodge Resort. This time he drove directly to Sunset Cottage, relieved that he saw no vehicles parked in front, no silver Mercedes or white Lexus. His relief lasted all of a few seconds. When he pulled into the parking lot in front of the cottage, he found its front door wide open. Not a good sign. He parked and climbed out of the Cherokee, pausing a moment. Should he get his Smith & Wesson out of the glove compartment? He decided against it, since there was no sign of the Doerings on the premises.

Fernando walked carefully through the garden and up to the porch. What he saw inside puzzled him. Two women from housekeeping were cleaning the cottage, top to bottom. One of them had pulled all the blankets and linen from the beds and piled everything on the floor of the bedroom. The other was cleaning the kitchen sink and counters. No sign of Becca or any indication that someone was actually staying in the cottage.

He walked into the cottage and looked around, searching for any evidence Becca was still here. All the bags and suitcases that he'd seen here yesterday were gone. Everything.

"Can I help you?" the older of the two women asked. She threw the last of the bedclothes on the floor and stood staring at him, hands on her hips. A thin, beanpole of a woman with short curly red hair wearing jeans and a T-shirt, she looked like she meant business.

Fernando smiled, trying to keep their conversation civil. "Yeah, I'm looking for Becca, the young woman who was staying here. I'm supposed to pick her up and bring her home."

At that moment the other woman came out of the kitchen. "What's the matter now?" she asked, a younger woman with long blond hair wearing black tights and a skimpy halter top.

"I'm looking for Becca, the young woman who was staying here," Fernando repeated.

"Well, you're too late," the older woman said, not bothering to hide her impatience with Fernando's interruption. "She checked out bright and early this morning."

"Fuck!" Fernando cursed, not liking what he was hearing. Then he remembered he had company. Both women were staring at him and not in a friendly way. "Oh, sorry about my language, I'm just surprised. I was supposed to take her to her parents' house this morning between eight and eight thirty."

Both women continued to stare at him, as if wondering why he was telling them his tale of woe.

"Who did she leave with, do you know?" Fernando asked.

The older woman shook her head. "The front desk might know, we just work in housekeeping."

"Thanks...sorry to bother you," Fernando said, and walked out of the cottage. On the porch he took a few deep breaths to calm himself. One thing after another. It just kept getting worse.

Sucking it up, he climbed back in the Cherokee and drove around the main loop to the office. Inside he found the reception desk jammed with tourists checking out of the resort. He had to wait in line for a good fifteen minutes before a desk clerk became available.

"Can I help you?" a kindly looking woman asked, flashing a big smile. She wore a name tag that read "Betty" clipped to her red silk blouse.

"Yes, I'm looking for the young woman who was staying in the Sunset Cottage," Fernando said. "I was supposed to pick her up this morning, but I understand she's already checked out."

Now the woman eyed him suspiciously, as if he were some kind of pedophile. "Really? I don't know what's going on here, but the older woman who booked the cottage paid the bill this morning and checked her out. She said the younger woman was her niece, if I remember correctly. So who are you?"

Fernando nodded. "I'm a friend of the family. I must have misunderstood. I thought I was supposed to pick her up this morning and give her a ride home to her parents."

Betty glanced at the window overlooking Bishop's Lodge Road. "Well, you're too late. She left about an hour ago."

"Much obliged," Fernando said, turning and walking away from the reception desk. Outside, he leaned against the Cherokee watching the traffic shoot by on Bishop's Lodge Road, most of it going into the city. Tesuque residents going to work, he reckoned. What now?

Becca had flown the coop again, leaving him with more questions. Had she gone on her own free will or under pressure from the Doerings? And where the hell had she flown to now?

23

Fernando knew Athena Gallery didn't open until 10 a.m., so he drove up to his old office and parked in the lot near where his sign had been. He knew Ruby hadn't arrived yet because her Honda Accord wasn't in the lot, so he walked down the gravel path to his office and unlocked the door. As soon as he stepped inside he noticed the change. Everything was spotless. The windows and even the furniture shined like polished steel. Ruby must have had one of her cleaning crews do a number on the office. She'd even added a small sofa or loveseat over by the wall of windows that overlooked the Santa Fe River and East Alameda Street. For a moment he wondered if she'd rented the space to a new tenant and forgot to tell him. While he brooded, he heard the hum of his mini-fridge and went to take a look. Sure enough, Ruby had stocked the small refrigerator with bottles of water and cans of Modelo. She'd guessed correctly that he would return.

Feeling guilty for never paying Ruby any rent, Fernando decided he would insist on paying her something for use of the space. If, that is, he intended to actually use the space. He went back and forth, brooding on the pros and cons and never quite making up his mind. Could a 'fixer' actually set up an office and advertise their services? Knowing the crank calls he'd received when he was a private investigator, he imagined new cranks calling in to ask him to come fix their kitchen sinks and so forth. Ha, ha, very funny. So he nixed that idea. If he did use the office, he for damned sure wouldn't advertise his services.

Meanwhile, he waited impatiently for ten o'clock when all the galleries opened on Canyon Road. Then a few minutes after ten o'clock he locked up and walked down to Athena Gallery. He saw lights on inside the gallery, so he assumed Mary Margaret and Angelica had opened. The bell rang loudly when he stepped inside. Mary Margaret stood at the counter, doing something with the cash register. He didn't see Angelica anywhere in the front of the gallery.

Excited to see him, Mary Margaret looked up at Fernando and smiled. "Did you find Becca?"

Fernando nodded. "Yeah, I found her at Bishop's Lodge Resort, where the Doerings had taken her to recover from a medical abortion. Did you know that Sonny had gotten her pregnant?"

"No!" Mary Margaret exclaimed. "Oh my God, why didn't she tell us? I don't understand. Is she all right?"

"I think so, but...," Fernando started to say but stopped when he heard Angelica yelling in back.

"So that's why she's missed so much time at work," Angelica said, coming in from the back room, not a happy smile on her face.

"Apparently," Fernando said. "Looked to me like the Doerings were holding her captive at Bishop's Lodge, trying to prevent her from talking about the abortion. I made arrangements with Becca to pick her up this morning and take her to her parents' house, but when I got there she was already gone. I think the Doerings moved her to a different location."

Both Mary Margaret and Angelica stared at him, neither speaking. Finally Mary Margaret leaned back against the counter and asked, "Why? Why would they be holding her captive? Just to keep the abortion secret?"

"Looks like it," Fernando said, walking to the counter to join the two women. "They insisted on the abortion and then kept Becca hidden at Bishop's Lodge Resort. They might have been afraid of a paternity test...in case Becca had any ideas about suing for part of the estate or whatever."

"Hmmm...that does sound like Athena," Mary Margaret said. "Got to protect her money."

"That's for sure, Athena loves her money, a lot more than Sonny ever did," Angelica added. "Sonny was just a careless drunk, he really didn't care about the money."

They stood in silence looking at each other for a long moment.

"Jesus, do you think they could harm Becca," Angelica asked finally. "I mean, maybe even kill her like they did Sonny?"

"Don't say that, please!" Mary Margaret shot back. "You don't know that for sure."

"Why not say it? I know they killed Sonny!" Angelica insisted.

Fernando sighed. "I don't know what they'll do next, but I'd like to find Becca before they do it. Do you have any idea where they could take her? Athena and Tom are staying at La Fonda, right?"

Angelica nodded.

"But I can't imagine them taking Becca to La Fonda," Fernando said. "Too public. Too many people around who would notice if they tried to hold anyone captive there."

Mary Margaret whispered something to Angelica, who nodded. Turning back to Fernando, Mary Margaret said, "Well, Athena owns a big house just off Hyde Park Road. That's where she and Sonny lived back when they were married. Athena's been staying at La Fonda, but she and Tom could have opened the Hyde Park house. It's been on the market now for months. It hasn't sold, probably because she was asking way too much for it."

"Almost four million dollars," Angelica added.

"Yeah, but just this week Athena reduced the price to three-point-five million," Mary Margaret said. "Now she wants a quick sale. She and her real estate agent have had a couple of open houses so far. I know Athena's been spending time there, making sure it's showable."

Fernando nodded. "Where exactly is this four million dollar house? Or should I say mansion?"

"It's on South Summit Drive, which is off Hyde Park Road just before you get to the Ten Thousand Waves spa," Angelica said. She wrote the address on a slip of paper and handed it to Fernando.

Fernando placed the paper in his shirt pocket. "So you've both been to this house?"

Mary Margaret nodded.

"A few times, mostly for parties and receptions for the artists when new shows opened at the gallery," Angelica said. "It is a real mansion, like most of the houses up there. At least for most of us."

"Yeah, but Athena's not most of us, is she?" Fernando said, mostly to himself. Like the rest of the filthy rich, the Doerings thought they could get away with anything. And they probably could. That was the problem.

"Are you okay?" Mary Margaret asked, noticing Fernando's sudden mood change.

"Not really," he said, checking his watch.

With that Fernando left the gallery. He hesitated before getting into his Cherokee, trying to think of a plan. At the moment his mind was blank.

Finally he climbed into the Cherokee and drove off down Canyon Road. As he approached Blaine's Picasso and Company gallery he spotted Blaine out front taking photos with his cell phone camera. Photos of the front of his gallery.

Confused, Fernando slowed down. Was Blaine planning to sell his gallery too, even after he'd invited Tessa to merge her gallery with his? Didn't make any sense. Not one bit.

He pulled into the parking lot off to the side of Picasso and Company. Then he buzzed down the window and honked. "Don't tell me you're selling too!" he shouted to Blaine, who walked over to the Cherokee.

Blaine shook his head, wearing his usual red Bermuda shorts and white T-shirt, sans fishing vest today. "No way. I'm trying to figure out what to do about our new sign—or maybe signs. Should we have separate signs, or should we include the names of both galleries on one sign? I want one sign, but Tessa wants separate signs. She says Picasso and Company is a pretentious, misleading, and stupid name for a gallery and she doesn't want to be associated with it."

Fernando laughed. "Sounds like Tessa."

"Yeah, but one sign would save us some money," Blaine said. "Plus I don't know if there's room on the front of the gallery to have two signs. It might look junky, like a goddamn pawn shop or something. That's all I need—for my Picasso and Company to look like a fucking pawn shop, you know? I sell real art, not just tourist shit and Jimmy Mackey's 'Chopped Nudes' crap."

Knowing Blaine's high opinion of himself and the art he collected in his gallery, Fernando chose to avoid the subject. "So what's Tessa going to call her gallery now that she's moved it to Santa Fe?" Fernando asked. "She can't very well keep 'Abiquiu Fine Art.'"

"Don't know yet," Blaine responded. "She says she hasn't decided on a name, only that it won't be stupid like Picasso and Company. Maybe something like 'Northern New Mexico Fine Art.'"

"Well, good luck," Fernando said. He was tired of hearing about the happy couple's problems.

Suddenly an idea occurred to Fernando. He cut the Cherokee's engine and stepped out of the vehicle. "Listen, I could use your help with something. I need to find Becca, who's apparently being held against her will by the Doerings. I don't know exactly why yet, but they're trying to keep Becca hidden away. Maybe because Becca just had an abortion, thanks to Sonny's philandering, and they don't want it to become public. Or maybe for some more sinister reason, I don't know, but I intend to find out. Will you help me?"

"Sonny knocked her up? That bastard!" Blaine said. "I should have taken him to the woodshed when I had the chance."

"Yeah, well, someone beat you to it," Fernando replied.

Frowning, Blaine shook his head. "Do you really think Becca's been kidnapped by the Doerings?"

"Well, maybe kidnapped is too strong a word," Fernando admitted. "Hidden away might be better."

"Okay, but do you have any idea where the Doerings are keeping her?" Blaine asked.

Fernando nodded. "They took her to a cottage at Bishop's Lodge Resort after the abortion. I found her there and made arrangements to pick her up this morning and take her to her parent's house, but they'd already moved her by the time I got there. Mary Margaret and Angelica think they may have taken her to Athena's old house on Hyde Park Road."

"You mean the house where Athena and Sonny lived before their divorce?" Blaine asked. "Yeah, I've been there for receptions. It's on South Summit Drive up by that fancy spa."

"Will you help me check it out?" Fernando asked.

Blaine sighed. "Okay...I suppose. You want me to go get my Beretta?"

Fernando shook his head. "No! No guns. I'm tired of shooting people and getting shot at. The fewer guns the better."

Blaine shot Fernando a puzzled look. "That's an odd thing for you to say...but, hey, suit yourself."

24

Blaine sat quietly in the passenger's seat and didn't say a word until Fernando turned onto Hyde Park Road. Then he glanced at Fernando and asked, "What did you mean back there when you said you were tired of shooting people? I thought that's what you do for a living: shoot people."

Fernando frowned. "I meant what I said. I'm tired of it. And anyway, these people aren't criminals, they're lawyers and art gallery owners. We won't need guns to deal with them."

"Hah! You don't fool me. I bet you have your Smith and Wesson locked in the glove compartment here," Blaine said, smacking the dash with his big palm.

Fernando laughed. "Well, just in case."

The further they traveled up Hyde Park Road, the more expensive the houses became. One million, two million, three million, cha-ching! For someone who'd lived in Santa Fe all his life, it was hard for Fernando to wrap his mind around the prices the over-class had brought to this once quaint, livable city. The sight of some of these monstrosities marring the beauty of the pine and aspen forested foothills caused Fernando to shake his head. The blight of gentrification had ruined the city for the locals, most of whom could no longer afford to live within the city limits, thanks to sky-rocketing housing costs and property taxes.

Trying to shake off his usual doom and gloom, Fernando slowed down approaching South Summit Drive. He turned right and asked, "How far down is the Doering house?"

"Go around the long curve and then look down to your right," Blaine said. "It's not too far beyond the curve."

Fernando did as he was told, slowing down even more to let an impatient Audi pass him on the curve. The Audi had to be going at least 60 mph, maybe more. On a curve.

"There!" Blaine said, pointing to the right side of the road, where South Summit Drive curved down into a small valley between the road and a series of rolling green hills that climbed the far side of the valley. "The Doering house is the first one you come to in the valley."

Fernando hit the brake and slowed the Cherokee looking for somewhere to pull over. When he saw the driveway of the first house on South Summit Drive he slowed to a stop and killed the engine. Below them they saw a sprawling multi-level house surrounded by a curving wall, the brown stucco of the building and the wall contrasting with the green hills. The lower level of the house extended out in two separate wings, one of them a linked series of three garages and the other what appeared to be a couple of attached guest quarters. The central, upper level of the house looked out over the foothills through banks of large windows, an entire floor of sunrooms. The only structure Fernando could compare it to was the crazy Mabel Dodge Luhan House in Taos, where the case of the missing Santa Fe historian had taken him a couple of years ago. The Mabel Dodge Luhan House was both historic and haunted, whereas this house looked new, sterile, and sloppily constructed. It was what you got these days for three or four million dollars.

"So this is how the over-class lives," Fernando said.

"It's a nightmare to keep up because of the shoddy construction," Blaine replied. "Athena's been trying to unload it for almost a year now. The fucking wood siding is rotting and the roof is leaking like a motherfucker, especially the skylights. It's a tough climate up here, with all the rain and snow during the winter. Would cost a pretty penny to repair."

"Looks like the whole gang's here," Fernando said, pointing to Athena's white Lexus and Tom's silver Mercedes, both parked near the triple garages. "Probably Becca too."

Blaine studied the layout. "How do you want to do this?"

"Let's take a closer look," Fernando said, taking his binoculars out of the glove compartment, next to his Smith & Wesson. He climbed out of the Cherokee and moved to the far side of the road to get a better look at the house below. He noticed the windows and patio doors on the upper level were all open, another indication that everyone was inside.

Fernando handed the binoculars to Blaine, who walked a few paces closer to the house and studied the layout. "What's this? Fuck me! Becca's in the first patio over there sunbathing."

Fernando grabbed the binoculars from Blaine. He looked at the patio behind the guest quarters at the end of the wing. Sure enough, a topless Becca lay on a chaise sunbathing, much as he'd seen her sunbathing at Bishop's Lodge Resort, except without her bikini top here. "No kidding," he mumbled to himself. She certainly didn't look like a kidnapped damsel in distress. More like a privileged young woman relaxing at an expensive spa.

"I don't know, Fernando, she sure doesn't look kidnapped to me," Blaine said finally. "Look at her, she's living the high life. The little bitch is probably in cahoots with them."

Fernando didn't answer. Instead, he put the binoculars back in the Cherokee and locked the doors. Then he started walking down the driveway toward the house. Blaine followed a few steps behind.

"Where are you going? You just gonna walk right in?" Blaine yelled, trying to keep up.

Fernando stopped. "You have a better plan?"

"Yeah, as a matter of fact I do," Blaine said. "Get your fucking Smith & Wesson out of the glove compartment. These guys could be armed. You don't know what the hell they're packing down there."

Fernando shrugged and continued walking down the rough asphalt driveway, not terribly worried about Tom and Ray.

The driveway curved sharply to the left and followed a faux adobe wall of cinderblocks and brown stucco that circled the property. They walked to the end of the wall and entered a large courtyard area, with a spraying water fountain in its center, pinched on either side by the two wings of the house. The central part of the house with its large banks of windows lay straight ahead at the end of the courtyard.

When they reached a walled patio behind the first guest quarters,

Fernando pointed to a wooden gate in the waist-high wall.

"I see it," Blaine said, still lagging behind.

Fernando opened the gate and entered the patio surprising Becca, whose body jerked in her seat. She lay topless on her chaise, wearing the floppy straw hat and heart-shaped sunglasses he'd seen her wear at Bishop's Lodge Resort. A real Lolita type, if that was a type these days. Becca did a double-take and removed her sunglasses. She stared at them curiously, as if they were totally out of place, like a couple of hillbillies crashing a formal reception.

Fernando saluted.

"Mister Lopez, what are you doing here?" Becca asked.

"I could ask you the same thing," Fernando responded, not pleased at this turn of events. "I was supposed to pick you up this morning and take you to your parents' house, remember?"

"Yeah, change of plan," Becca said, making no effort to explain or to cover her breasts.

"So what are you doing here?" Fernando asked.

"Just chillin'," Becca replied. "They're trying to keep me as far away as possible from Sonny's murder investigation."

Fernando shook his head, confused. He didn't know what to make of her last statement, so he said, "From what I'm told, you don't have much to worry about. I don't think they have enough evidence to charge anyone."

Becca smiled. She seemed happy, unreasonably so, given the circumstances, Fernando thought.

Just then Blaine entered the patio. He froze when he spotted Becca lying on the chaise. "Whoa...now we're talking."

Fernando elbowed the big man, who looked like he was about to lick his lips. "Remember Tessa, your true love?"

"Who?" Blaine shot back, never taking his eyes off Becca's perfectly round, pointed breasts.

"How old are you now, Becca?" Blaine asked.

"I'll be twenty next month," Becca said.

Fernando elbowed Blaine again. "You're fucking incorrigible, Blaine."

Blaine turned to Fernando. "Just keeping my options open."

Fernando decided to ignore Blaine. He walked over to Becca. "I guess I don't understand what's going on. Do you want to get out of here or not? You can come with us now, if you want."

Becca seemed confused. She looked around, as if searching for help. "I don't know." She stood up and slowly pulled on a T-shirt over her bare breasts. "Let's talk to Athena...see what she thinks."

Blaine frowned when her breasts disappeared under the T-shirt. He shook his head sadly.

Becca led the way, walking across the patio to the door into the guest quarters. She opened the door and suddenly Roy, Tom's stooge, brushed past Becca onto the patio. In his right hand Roy held a small Ruger LCP, a nasty little gun that could make a nasty large hole.

"Awww, shit! What did I tell you!" Blaine barked, pissed that Fernando had left his Smith & Wesson in the Cherokee.

Roy pointed his pistol directly at Fernando's forehead.

25

"You're trespassing! I could shoot you under the 'Stand your Ground law,'" Roy said.

"New Mexico doesn't have a Stand Your Ground law," Fernando said. "And we're not armed, so you can't claim you're being threatened. You're out of your league, Roy."

Impulsive as always, Blaine brushed Fernando aside. "Put the fucking gun down before I take it away from you and shove it up your ass!" Blaine said, towering over Roy, who was a good six inches shorter and seventy-five pounds lighter than Blaine.

Roy backed away from Blaine, clearly intimidated by what appeared to be a crazy man. "You have a big mouth. Maybe I'll shoot you first."

"Definitely shoot him first," Fernando said.

Blaine gave Fernando a dirty look.

"Maybe I will," Roy said, pointing the gun at Blaine.

"Wait!" Fernando said, noticing Blaine moving toward Roy. He managed to get between them and push Blaine back away from Roy. He didn't want Roy to get mauled by Blaine or Blaine to get shot in some macho struggle over the Ruger. "I want you to take us to Athena. We need to talk."

"You heard the man," Blaine barked.

Roy hesitated a moment and then motioned for them to enter the guest quarters. They walked through a large bedroom suite with a bath and small sitting area—a sofa and two Queen Anne chairs arranged around an expensive looking oriental rug. The place looked nearly as affluent as Bishop's Lodge Resort, just not as well kept up.

Once outside in the central courtyard Blaine took off walking fast toward the main house at the end of the courtyard. The big man had been here before and knew exactly where to find Athena. Fernando and Roy, still waving his Ruger, fell quickly behind Blaine, with Roy shouting loudly, "Hey. Where do you think you're going? Wait up!"

Becca followed at a leisurely pace, bringing up the rear. She seemed slightly amused by the entire scene. At one point she laughed when Roy stumbled on the flagstone walkway trying to catch Blaine.

Going on ahead, Blaine burst into the main house. The big man walked into a large foyer, overgrown with so many potted plants that it resembled a jungle. He didn't hesitate, stomping up a polished wooden stairway to a sunroom on the upper level, where Athena was sprawled out on a leather sofa, looking relaxed. Tom, on the other hand, was pacing back and forth by the bank of windows that overlooked the forested hills outside, looking anything but relaxed. Both turned to look at Blaine, not so much surprised as disappointed.

Then Roy fought his way into the sunroom waving his Ruger. "I found them on the patio with Becca," Roy said, out of breath. "I think they were trying to convince her to leave with them."

Fernando and Becca followed and watched the scene unfold from the top of the stairway.

"Yeah, I saw them from the window," Tom said, disgusted.

Athena sighed. "Mister Lopez, what do you want? Why do you continue with this? I told you I would pay you fifty thousand dollars if you would just disappear and leave us alone!"

"I want some answers," Fernando said bluntly.

"Why? Why do you care about what happened to Sonny?" Athena asked. "You helped me get rid of him once, why not again? As I recall, you even threatened him with a gun."

"I helped you persuade him to sign divorce papers, not to kill him," Fernando said. "There's a difference."

"Why does it matter?" Athena shot back. "He was a despicable human being. You know this as well as anyone. You know his history of domestic abuse, his violence against women. Truly, there are simply no words to adequately describe the depth of his depravity."

Fernando stood back and held his tongue, letting Athena continue her rant. She was clearly enjoying her performance.

"You know he treated the young women he hired at the gallery as sex slaves that he could assault any time he pleased," Athena said bitterly. "And it wasn't only Mary Margaret and Angelica and Becca. You might not know this, but he was one of the degenerates who frequented Three Hills Ranch before it was raided. He had sex with the teenage girls Robert Warner was trafficking there."

Fernando nodded. He did indeed know about Robert Warner's Three Hills Ranch and that Sonny had been one of Warner's patrons. He'd been lead detective on the raid that busted Three Hills. One of his worst cases. He still had nightmares about finding the girls and Robert Warner's helicopter bursting into flames when he tried to flee and instead careened into the hillside.

"That was why I filed for divorce," Athena continued. "The very day I found out he was frequenting Three Hills, I called my lawyer. I wanted nothing more to do with Sonny. I kicked him out of my house and told him I would never have anything to do with him, ever."

"Save your breath. I feel the same way you do about Sonny. I don't give a damn about him—or you, for that matter," Fernando said. "I just want to make sure none of my friends are charged with a murder you committed."

Athena glared at him. "I told you, I didn't kill Sonny. I was still in Cincinnati when he was murdered."

The room fell silent.

Tom stopped pacing by the bank of windows.

Roy lowered his Ruger and tucked the gun into his shoulder holster.

Suddenly Becca cleared her throat and took a seat next to Athena on the leather sofa. "I shot him!" she announced loudly. She turned to Athena. "Either you tell him or I will."

Everyone stared at Becca.

"Be careful," Tom cautioned finally, assuming the role of Becca's lawyer.

"I just couldn't take it anymore, him grabbing me and expecting me to have sex with him whenever and wherever he wanted it. And then when I got pregnant he said he was sorry he couldn't have had me spayed like his dogs. I felt so insulted, so dehumanized. I couldn't take it any more."

Becca stopped for a moment and glanced at Athena, who shook her head no, as if warning Becca not to continue. Becca ignored her.

"So when Athena offered to pay for my abortion and give me one hundred thousand dollars, I said yes," Becca said, continuing in spite of Athena's warning. "I found the gun and the bullets in Sonny's desk and took them home after work that night. Then I loaded the gun and waited until later. I knew Sonny was hooking up with someone he met at the La Fonda bar, so I came back to the office about ten o'clock and let myself in. Sonny was all disheveled, still on the Taos sofa in his office where he liked to fuck us. He had a video camera on the bookshelf, which he used to film us whenever he did something out of the ordinary. He liked to come up with new positions or movements. Sometimes he would show the videos to friends in his soccer club for laughs. All of them thought the tapes were funny. On occasion he would invite one of his friends to join him in a session, a three-way. Not with me, but with the others. I refused that, at least. I started to hate him for what he did to us, so when Athena offered me the money, I said yes. I wanted him dead."

When Becca finished, the silence was deafening. No one spoke.

Athena lowered her head. Tom sat down in a chair across from Athena and Becca. Roy quietly retreated out of the room, walking back down the stairs and disappearing. Fernando and Blaine stood frozen beside the sofa, staring at Becca and Athena, both of whom were surprisingly calm The ugly truth was out, never to be put back in the bottle.

Finally Athena sighed and shook her head sadly. "There you have it. Happy now?" she asked Fernando. "That's what you want, right? The answer you've been seeking?"

"And I don't care, I'm not sorry!" Becca blurted out and then buried her head in her hands, weeping.

Now everyone stared at Fernando, seeming to blame him for Becca's weeping. As if he were the bad guy here. The villain.

Tom stood up and faced Fernando. "So you see, if you continue to pursue this and Becca and/or Athena is charged, we will be forced to bring in all the sexcapades and the videos and everyone involved in them," he said to Fernando. "You'd be surprised at some of the names I could give you. It will be messy, very messy. A lot of lives will be ruined, including Becca's and Mary Margaret's and Angelica's. Trust me, Santa Fe will never be the same."

Again, no one spoke.

Fernando glanced at Blaine and then moved closer to the sofa. He put his hand on a sobbing Becca's shoulder and gave it a squeeze. Then he turned to Athena and said, "Take good care of Becca. If you don't, you will be hearing from me again."

With that, Fernando turned and walked out of the sunroom and down the stairs. He heard Blaine following along behind, his 250-pound body clomping on the wooden steps.

Once outside Fernando threw his arms up above his head, reaching for the sky and stretching his muscles. He took a deep breath and began the long walk back to his Cherokee.

Blaine caught him halfway up the hill. "What are you going to do now?"

"Nothing," Fernando said. "Absolutely nothing."

26

One morning a couple of weeks later Fernando waited until Estelle left for work and then drove down to Ruby's gallery on Canyon Road. He'd given the key to his former office back to Ruby, deciding that it was ridiculous to go to an empty office every morning just to read his newspaper and twiddle his thumbs. Instead, every weekday morning he went down to Ruby's gallery to drink coffee and read the newspapers. That way he could still hang out with his Canyon Road friends: Ruby, Tessa, Blaine, Paul and June Bryan at Essentia next door, and even old Dave Stein, who despite his age appeared at El Farol every afternoon for happy hour.

This morning Ruby greeted him from the counter that Ruby referred to as the lunchroom, where she'd just made a pot of coffee. "Lots of news today," she said, handing him a cup of coffee as he took a seat at the counter. Ruby looked like a million bucks today, wearing black tights and a slinky rose-colored blouse that was cut dangerously low. Admiring her now, he had a flashback to when they were both in Santa Fe High and he had a mad crush on her, a million years ago.

"Good or bad news?" Fernando asked, accepting the steaming hot cup of coffee and reaching for the cream and sugar.

"Athena stopped in a few minutes ago on her way to the airport in Albuquerque," Ruby said. "She sold her gallery. Or at least she has a contract to sell it. The buyers are a married gay couple from Los Angeles who also bought a house up by Saint John's College. They say they're happy to be moving to Santa Fe, where the prices are half what they are in L.A. Can you believe that?"

Fernando laughed. "I can imagine. Instead of four million in L.A., a mere two million in Santa Fe."

"Pisses me off," Ruby said. "I still live in that efficiency apartment attached to my pottery co-op."

"Gentrification," Fernando said. "We lost the war, remember? By the way, did Athena sell her house on Hyde Park Road?"

"Not yet," Ruby replied. "Apparently it needs some work. She lowered the price to two point five million."

"Bargain basement price!" Fernando joked.

"Hey...maybe it'll sink to my range, one hundred grand tops!"

While they talked, they heard the front door of the gallery open and the loud booming voice of Blaine. "Hell no! I'm not gonna stop drinking! I don't drink any more than your sister! Ask her if you don't believe me!"

"Yer full of shit!" Tessa countered, shoving Blaine through the door into the lunchroom.

"Now what?" Ruby asked. "One day I see you two all lovey-dovey and the next you're fighting like a couple of pit bulls."

Tessa looked younger than ever, wearing cutoff jean shorts and a sleeveless top. She poked Blaine in the back. "It's him, he drinks too much. Every day he has to go to El Farol for happy hour and get smashed. Half the time he's no good in bed because he's smashed!" she yelled.

Wait a damn minute...." Blaine started.

"Same thing I told him a few years back when we were hanging out," Ruby interrupted. "He can't hold his liquor, he's a sloppy drunk."

'Hah! I don't drink as much as you," Blaine said to Ruby. "And I can still drink you under the table, no matter what you say.

"You see?" Tessa said to Ruby. "He won't listen. You can't get through to him. It's like talking to a fucking door!"

Fernando raised his hands high over his head, calling for a truce. "Well, I'm glad you two are getting along so well, but what else is new? Did you order the new sign for your two galleries?"

Tessa nodded. "Yeah, but the name of his gallery is bigger than the name of my gallery on the sign."

Blaine shook his head. "I give up. So what's new with you guys?"

"Plenty," Ruby said. She told them about Athena's visit, that Athena had sold her gallery but not her house. Then she told them about the new owners of the gallery from L.A.

"What about the girls, Becca and Angelica and Mary Margaret?" Blaine asked. "Becca's hot! Great looking boobs!"

Tessa elbowed Blaine in the gut. "When did you see her boobs?"

"Owww," Blaine hollered. "When we went over to talk to Athena at her house on Hyde Park Road, I told you. Becca was sunbathing topless."

Tessa made a face at Blaine.

"Sorry Blaine, but Becca took the one hundred grand Athena gave her and moved back to Albuquerque," Ruby said. "She re-enrolled at UNM and rented an apartment near campus. She's finishing her undergraduate degree this semester and plans to enroll in the College of Pharmacy next semester. I don't know about Mary Margaret and Angelica. Maybe they'll continue working for the new owners."

"Did you say pharmacy?" Blaine asked, raising an eyebrow. "Now you're talking. Becca's looking better all the time."

Tessa gave Blaine the Evil Eye.

"Good for her, she deserves a break," Fernando said.

"Yeah, and Sonny got what he deserves too," Ruby added.

Tessa shook herself free and stepped away from Blaine. "So who killed Sonny? No one's ever told me. Or doesn't anyone know?"

Fernando nodded at Blaine. He was pleased that Blaine hadn't told Tessa what they'd learned at Athena's house on Hyde Park Road. Blaine had kept their vow of silence, their decision not to tell who murdered Sonny, as had Fernando. Not a soul.

"What? No one knows?" Tessa asked again.

Fernando smiled. "It was a group effort."

Ruby nodded her agreement. "We all killed Sonny. Or wanted to."

READERS GUIDE

1. Former Santa Fe Police Detective Fernando Lopez now calls himself a 'fixer.' How does Fernando describe the role of a 'fixer'? What does he fix?

2. Why is Sonny Davis shot and killed in the very first chapter that we will learn more about later?

3. Why is Fernando's longtime friend Ruby Montez initially the number one suspect in the Sonny Davis murder?

4. How does Fernando get involved with Tessa Montez, Ruby's younger sister? What history do they share?

5. How would you describe Tessa's relationship with Blaine Rogers, the owner of the Picasso and Company gallery in Santa Fe? How does their relationship change in the course of the story?

6. Fernando first helps Tessa at her gallery in Abiquiu. What does he learn about her situation in Abiquiu? Explain.

7. One afternoon Fernando is surprised to find Sonny Davis' ex-wife Athena Doering at El Farol. How does Fernando know Athena? What is their history? Why has she come back to Santa Fe?

8. Who is Raoul Garcia? What advice does Raoul give Fernando that helps unravel the case?

9. When Fernando interviews the three young women who worked for Sonny what picture of Sonny begins to emerge? In particular, how do Mary Margaret, Angelica, and Becca describe Sonny? Why do they put up with Sonny's treatment? What does Fernando learn about the murder instrument from talking to them?

10. While helping protect Tessa from her Abiquiu neighbor Ray Sandoval, Fernando ends up spending a night in her casita at the Ojo Caliente hot springs. Does he sleep with Tessa?

11. Who is Ray Sandoval? What's his grudge against Tessa? How do Blaine and Fernando resolve the situation?

12. When Fernando finally interviews Becca, the youngest of the women who worked for Sonny, Fernando learns more about the murder weapon and the killing. What else does Fernando learn from Becca that helps him solve the case?

13. Mary Margaret contacts Fernando and asks him to meet her. What does Fernando learn from Mary Margaret about Becca and Sonny's relationship?

14. Why has Athena Doering brought her brother Tom with her to Santa Fe? Why does he try to intimidate Fernando, telling Fernando to back off his investigation?

15. Who informs Fernando that Becca has gone missing? What action do the two of them take to find Becca? How does Fernando find Becca at Bishop's Lodge?

16. Who has kidnapped Becca? Why are they holding her at Bishop's Lodge?

17. What does Becca tell Fernando when he finds her alone at Bishop's lodge that begins to unlock the secret of who killed Sonny?

18. Fernando arranges to help Becca escape her confinement, but when he arrives at Bishop's Lodge to pick her up she's gone. Athena and Tom have taken her away. How does Fernando find out where the Doerings are holding Becca?

19. Fernando enlists the help of Blaine Rogers to rescue Becca. Where do they find Becca?

20. When Fernando and Blaine find Becca, they uncover the secret of Sonny's killing. They learn who, how, and why Sonny was murdered. Explain? What does Fernando intend to do with this knowledge?